# When the Angel of Death Tells Bedtime Stories

## By Sabine Meyer

For Lael, my good friend and mentor.

Book Cover and illustrations by Sabine Meyer. Artificial intelligence was used to aid in the generation of the artwork. Programs used included Gemini and Fotor.

Second edition 2025

ISBN 979-8-9993430-1-7

# TABLE OF CONTENTS

## PART ONE: BEDTIME STORIES FOR FANNY     5


The Little Dog Who Became a Volcano ..................8

The Bad Mom ..................17

The Multidimensional Boy ..................32

Hansel and Gretel ..................40

Veritas ..................46

The Lellek ..................55

The Worm of Disorder ..................67

Hair ..................74

Fanny and the Two-Headed Dragon ..................86

The Fight with the Red Snake ..................95


## PART TWO: MICHAEL     101


In the Beginning ..................103

Young Michael ..................109

The Flight Across Two Oceans ..................118

The Slaughter of the Angels ..................124

The Last of the Angels ..................132

Lost Souls ..................139

The Falling Angel ..................143


## PART THREE: FANNY'S FAMILY STORY     149

Jeema .......................................................................... 151

Godfather Death .......................................................... 157

No Torture Can Last Forever ...................................... 164

The Stoneking's Wife .................................................. 168

The Stoneking's Daughter ........................................... 175

The Stoneking's Origin ............................................... 179

Rowena's Baby ........................................................... 185

Little Boats Adrift ...................................................... 198


## PART FOUR: FANNY GROWS UP       205


Linnea and the Seven Firefighters ................................ 207

The Woman Who Wanted Her Husband Back ............... 220

The Vampire Who Was Allergic to Blood ..................... 234

The Girl Who Loved Creepy-Crawlies ......................... 253


## PART FIVE: REDEMPTION       273


The Kiss of Death ....................................................... 274

The Devil's Apprentice ............................................... 279

Judgment Day ............................................................ 289

# PART ONE: BEDTIME STORIES FOR FANNY

*Michael poked his head through the door and smiled at Fanny.*

*"Ready?" he asked.*

*Fanny was five, a green-eyed girl with blonde locks and two dimples. Grandma had tucked her in securely, and now it was story time.*

*Michael, pronounced "Mee-kha-El," was Fanny's godfather. He was also the Angel of Death. He appeared as a dark young man with raven-black wings and ebony hair, but he had light-filled, blue eyes.*

*Fanny and Grandma Diana were his family – as much as an angel could have a family, that is. Michael grabbed the heavy tome of fairy tales from the table and plopped into the red armchair next to Fanny's bed.*

*"You look like a little cherub," Michael remarked.*

*"What's a cherub?"*

*"A baby angel. You remind me of my brothers when they were little. Imagine a flock of two hundred young angels, all with blonde hair and fluffy white wings."*

*Fanny's eyes widened.*

*"Two hundred brothers?"*

*"They were Angels of Light. When they descended from the sky, the glow of their wings turned night into day. When they flew in formation, they made a deafening sound like a million hornets. When they sang, Earth herself stood still and listened."*

*Michael hesitated, then he added, "They are all gone now. The snake ate them."*

*The last of the setting sun disappeared below the horizon. A gust of cold air came through the open bedroom window.*

*Fanny's lower lip quivered. "Did that happen a long, long time ago?"*

*"Yes, a very long time ago, when humankind was young. But I still miss them."*

*"I wish I could hug you," Fanny said.*

*"Me too," Michael smiled at the girl. "But you know I can't. My touch brings death, and you are supposed to stay alive for many more years."*

*For the ten thousand years of his life, Michael had walked the Earth unseen and unheard, quietly collecting his souls. Then he met Hannah, who was unique among humans in that she could see him.*

*Michael still felt guilty about Hannah, but he did not want to think about that right now. His thoughts drifted. What he longed for was a soul-to-soul connection, but he had no soul, so he could not connect, not really. His little extravaganza with this human family was a luxury he allowed himself, for as long as it lasted.*

*Michael tore himself away from his musings and asked, "Which one do you want to hear tonight? The one with the wolf and the little girl in red clothes?"*

*"That's Little Red Riding Hood," said Fanny. "No, tell me one that's not in the book, maybe one about someone lonely?"*

*"No problem," said the Angel of Death. "I'll tell you the story of the little dog who became a volcano."*

# Chapter One

# The Little Dog Who Became a Volcano

Once upon a time, there was a puppy who lived in a spacious house with a warm fireplace, a fine kitchen, and a lush garden. The owner of the house was a gnarly old man who had bought the puppy because he wanted a guard dog to protect his mansion from thieves.

Now, the puppy was young and not vicious at all, which displeased the old man. He took the puppy to a dog-training school so that his dog could learn to be fierce. The puppy met many big dogs at that school. They had powerful jaws and sharp teeth, and when they growled, the windows shook. The puppy invited the big dogs to play by lifting his butt and wagging his tail, but they ignored him. If he was too insistent, they snapped at him.

The old man was not here to play. "Fass," he yelled at the puppy, holding out a thick pad on his arm.

The puppy could not bring himself to bite the old man and hung his head in shame.

After many fruitless days at the dog-training school, the old man devised a different plan. He restricted the puppy's food to one-quarter cup of dry dog food every day, hoping that hunger would turn the puppy into the nasty guard dog he wanted.

Meanwhile, the man cooked all kinds of good food for himself: fried fish, grilled chicken, pot roast, and lamb chops. The little dog sniffed up all the delicious smells coming from the man's stove. He whined and pleaded for just one little piece, made his best puppy eyes, and rolled on the floor to show his soft belly, but the old man never shared anything, not one little bite.

One night, the puppy could not take it any longer. He snuck into the kitchen and opened the garbage can. There, he found a chicken bone, and he gobbled it up.

The old man never noticed a thing, so the next night, the puppy slipped into the kitchen again and raided the waste basket, being careful to clean up very well when he was done. That went on for several nights, but soon, the little dog got tired of bones without any meat on them, so he opened the refrigerator. He found some chicken nuggets on a plate, snatched one, and swallowed it in one gulp.

The next day, the old man was puzzled, thinking he had made six chicken nuggets, but now there were only five. Then, he shrugged and told himself he was getting old and forgetful.

From then on, the little dog went to the refrigerator every night. At first, he stole only little morsels of food, but he got bigger and hungrier, and one day, he took a whole chicken.

The old man had prepared the chicken for a party, so he was sure he had not eaten it. He looked around, wondering what had happened to it, and when he found pieces of bone near the little dog's bed, he knew.

"Bad dog!" he yelled. "This is how you thank me for feeding you and giving you shelter? OUT!"

The man banished the dog into the yard. The puppy was forced to sleep in a drafty doghouse and was left alone all day. All he had was a bowl of stale water and a dish holding a quarter cup of dry dog food.

Soon, the little dog became very hungry again, so when night came, he looked around the garden for things to eat. To his delight, he found rows of vegetables: peas, beans, zucchinis, and onions. He ate all the vegetables, and then he saw a patch of strawberries and blueberries. When he was done with the berries, he turned to the flowers in the garden. He gobbled up all the roses, spitting out the thorns, and devoured dahlias, petunias, and black-eyed Susans. Then he ate even the bushes and, finally, the lawn. He ripped out every blade of grass until only mud was left in place of the man's prized turf.

When the old man saw the disaster in his yard, he was furious. He beat the dog and put him on a chain so that he could walk only a few paces. The dog cried, but the old man paid him no attention, so the dog lay down next to his doghouse and whimpered to himself.

When darkness fell over the yard, the dog began to chew through the chain. He chomped and chomped, tore it into little pieces, and ate the whole thing. Then, he began to gnaw at the fence. When he was done with the fence, he got to work on the house, but then he heard the old man's angry voice from inside. The dog became frightened and ran.

He ran, and he ran until he reached a nearby village. There, he saw a big grocery store. The smell of all the goodies in that store made his mouth water. So, the dog waited until evening, and when the last people were leaving the store, he zipped through the door so fast that nobody noticed him.

Once in the store, the dog started to eat. First, he gobbled up all the meat and the fish, even the frozen ones. Then he found bananas, vegetables, bread, and cookies. He did not stop until he had devoured every single thing on the shelves, even the cans and the paper towels. And when the shelves were all bare, he ate the shelves, too.

When the people wanted to return to the store in the morning, they found that the door would not open. The reason was that the dog had gotten enormously big, so he was filling up the whole store. Eventually, the people called a construction crew, which removed the roof and lifted the big dog out of the building with the help of three large cranes.

The cranes transported the dog to a forest a hundred miles away, and there they left him, saying, "Bad dog. Don't you ever dare to come back."

The dog walked through the forest, eating everything in his path. Eventually, he became so heavy that Earth herself could no longer carry his weight. The dirt gave way under the dog's feet, and he sank into the deep. He sank lower and lower until he reached the core of the Earth, which was so hot that all the rock had melted into fiery, liquid magma. Soon, the dog got hungry again, so he swallowed some of the molten stone. This new food made the dog grow, and soon, he became so big that he pushed up a whole mountain. Every time the dog burped, there was an eruption of red-hot lava.

And thus, the dog remained for many years, imprisoned in a volcano of his own making, very alone, his stomach filled to the brim with lava.

The people in the vicinity of the volcano were not happy. The fiery eruptions were dangerous, so they never went very close. The dog had nobody to talk to and often cried himself to sleep. When he did that, a cloud of steam rose up from his crater.

But then, one day, the dog had a visitor. It was a young girl who had come to see the volcano. She sat down at the base of the big mountain to rest, and there, she heard a loud rumbling. It came from inside the mountain, and it sounded exactly like her own stomach when she was hungry.

"Mountain," she said. "Are you hungry?"

"I am always hungry," replied the dog.

"I'll share my sandwich with you," said the girl, and she placed half of her sandwich on the feet of the volcano.

The sandwich disappeared into the ground like a drop of water on dry sand.

"Thank you," said the dog. "That was good, but I am still hungry."

"I will be back tomorrow," said the girl.

From then on, the girl visited the dog every day. She always brought her lunch and shared it with the dog. As time went by, something strange happened to the volcano; it began to shrink.

"Are you OK?" asked the girl, worried the volcano might be sick. "I'll try to bring you more food."

The mountain gobbled up every crumb she gave him, but still, it shrank. Soon, it was only as tall as a skyscraper, then it shrank to the size of a house, and finally, it disappeared; instead, there was only a large, black egg. The egg was huge, as tall as the girl, and had a smooth shell of obsidian.

The girl put half of her sandwich on the ground, but the sandwich was not absorbed.

"Hm," said the girl. "Are you not hungry?"

"I am still hungry," said a voice inside the egg. "You have to put the food directly on my shell."

When the girl did that, the egg began to wobble and shake, and a piece of the eggshell fell off. The girl peered inside and laughed when something in there licked her face. She reached into the egg and pulled out a tiny puppy. It was all wet and had black eyes as big and shiny as marbles.

"What shall I do with you?" wondered the girl as she took off her jacket to pat the puppy dry. "Well, if you like, you can be my puppy forever."

The girl brought the puppy to her little house. The house had a small yard and was painted pink. The puppy loved everything about it. The girl shared all the food in her refrigerator with him. There were macaroni and cheese, arugula salad with goat cheese and pears, and about half a dozen peanut butter sandwiches. When night came, the puppy hopped on the girl's bed and went round and round until he had made himself a nice, cozy nest.

The dog and the girl lived together happily until one night, the dog sensed something that made him uneasy. The moon was full, and the mists were rising over the fields. The dog heard the coyotes howling in the distance;

he felt the silent swoop of an owl overhead. He lifted his ears and sniffed the air. And there it was, an evil scent, still a mile away. It was coming. It smelled of cigarettes, whiskey, and dirt. The dog growled under his breath and nudged the girl, who was sound asleep. The girl could not smell the evil thing in the distance, so she let the dog out, thinking he needed to pee.

The dog paced the yard. The scent was stronger now, and he could hear the voices of three men. Then, he saw them as they climbed over the fence. They were dressed in black clothes, wearing masks on their faces. They were carrying guns, knives, and a rope. The dog showed his teeth and gave a fierce snarl, but the burglars laughed.

"Look at that puppy," they said. "Hey, little puppy, do you want to be a guard dog when you grow up?"

The dog lunged at the burglars, and as he jumped, he became bigger, much bigger. When he landed on top of the intruders, he was as large as a truck.

The dog belched out a fiery stream of lava that set the burglars on fire and burned them to ashes in the blink of an eye. When the dog was sure that nothing was left of the thieves, he shrank to the size of a puppy again and whined at the back door until the girl let him in.

"Good puppy," said the girl. "You are shivering. Are you cold? Let's go back to our warm bed."

Fanny chuckled. *"Did the girl ever find out that her dog had superpowers?"*

*"I don't think so. The little dog was very discreet about his guard duties. Things got a little hairy when the girl started to date. The puppy would growl at all the men who came to the house. Once, when a man stayed overnight, the dog peed all over the man's bag."*

*"Oh no,"* said Fanny. *"Did she put him in the pound?"*

*"The dog?"* Michael asked incredulously. *"I want to see the girl who would give up her beloved pup for a man. No, the girl continued to look for a good man until she found one who met the puppy's approval."*

Fanny smiled at Michael. *"That girl had a guardian puppy; I have a guardian angel."*

Something inside Michael's chest bounced all of a sudden. It made his breathing difficult, and his heartbeat stumbled. If Michael could have chosen his calling, he would have been a guardian angel, not the Angel of Death. He would spread his protective wings over the child under his care. He would keep her safe and guide her until it was time for the Angel of Death to collect her soul. Then Michael would be assigned to another child and another, and slowly, the Space for Souls would become populated by souls who glowed with his blessings.

*"I was not made for that purpose,"* Michael said. *"But I am doing the best I can."*

*****

*A few days later, Fanny pointed to a picture book about dragons."*

*"Are dragons real?"* she wanted to know.

*"I have never met one," Michael said. "But I can tell you a story about a dragon – a terrifying beast."*

# Chapter Two

# The Bad Mom

Once upon a time, there was a Bad Mom. She was VERY bad. One evening, she came home to a huge mess in the living room. She had worked all day and was exhausted, cranky, and hungry. There were blocks and puzzle pieces, little toy cars, cookie crumbs, dirty diapers, and banana peels all over the carpet. The older kids' homework was crumpled up in one corner, and the dog had pooped on the pile of papers. There were also two empty beer bottles, a half-eaten tray of Chinese takeout, a pair of muddy men's shoes, and two mismatched, stinky socks. The mess was so dense that the Bad Mom could not walk across the living room without stepping on something sharp or disgusting.

So, she asked the kids to pick up their toys, and the kids cried that they did not know how. The Mom asked the kids' dad to show them how it was done.

"You are a bad mother," said the father. "I babysat all day so you could get your work done; the least you could do is clean up."

So, the Bad Mom grabbed a garbage bag, put all the toys and all the mess in it, and hauled it to the garbage dump. The kids' howling echoed all over the street.

Sometime later, she did eight loads of laundry. She worked on it for three hours, and then her back hurt, so she asked the kids to help with the folding. The kids said they didn't know how, and the father said the same thing.

The Bad Mom took two socks, rolled them together, and said: "Like this. It's easy. See?"

But while she was looking for matching socks, the kids and their dad walked out into the yard to play ball. The Bad Mom growled like an angry dog, then folded all of her own clothes and put the rest in a few big baskets, which she dumped on the damp basement floor. The next morning, the kids could not find anything to wear.

"Find something in the heap in the basement," said the Bad Mom.

"But I am scared to go into the basement," cried the middle child.

"All the clothes down there are smelling of mold," said the oldest.

The dad appeared in the kitchen wearing a stained and wrinkled shirt.

"I can't go to work this way," he complained. "My boss will kill me. You are a Bad Mom."

The next day, the Bad Mom was sewing. There were socks with holes in them, shirts with missing buttons, and pants with hems that had come undone. She sewed and sewed until the scissors slipped from her hands, and she stabbed herself in the hand. Her blood dripped on the floor.

The Bad Mom wrapped a sock around her hand and sat beside the window. High up in the sky, she saw a flock of geese winging their way North and calling to each other.

"I wish I could fly away with them," said the Bad Mom.

And with that, she got up from her chair and walked out into the world, slamming the door behind her.

At first, the dad and the kids could not believe she had left, but the dad knew what to do. He went to a discount store and got them a new mom. That one did not mind cleaning, tidying, doing laundry, and sewing from morning to night. She let the kids have as much candy as they wanted, and they were allowed to watch TV all day. Now, the kids and their father were content.

In the meantime, the Bad Mom walked and walked until she got to a dark forest. Before long, she was lost. It was cold; there was nothing to eat except some wild berries, and, worst of all, the Bad Mom could hear wolves howling in the distance. When night fell, she climbed a huge tree so the wolves wouldn't get her while she slept. She had never had a more awful night. When daybreak finally came, she got out of the tree, cramped and aching in every muscle. Her stomach rumbled, and she was cold and wet from the morning dew.

"I am surely going to die in these woods," she muttered, but there was no turning back, so she kept walking.

The Bad Mom trudged on for seven long days, sleeping in trees and gathering berries and roots for food.

On the eighth day, she stumbled upon a clearing. She turned her face to the sun and let its rays warm her shivering body. Then, she saw a small castle with a moat, two drawbridges, three little turrets, and a colorful flag. The Bad Mom sighed with happiness.

"I will find food in that castle," she thought. "Maybe even warm clothes. I will be able to rest, and the people in the castle can tell me how to get out of these cursed woods."

Alas, there was no easy way into the castle. The building had two gates; one was guarded by giant elephants, and the other was blocked by fierce lions. The Bad Mom tried to sneak by the animals, but the lions roared at her, baring their enormous, yellow fangs. The elephants lifted their trunks and trumpeted in her face, threatening her with their gleaming tusks. She pleaded and begged, but the animals did not allow her to pass.

So, she thought of a ruse. She picked up a few rocks and went up to the elephants. Then she yelled and threw her rocks at the animals. The stones had sharp edges, so the elephants squealed in pain and lumbered after the Bad Mom. Elephants can run very fast, but the Bad Mom had a head start and sprinted towards the lions' gate as fast as she could. The elephants were in hot pursuit and collided with the lions. It took a few minutes for the angry animals to sort things out, and meanwhile, the Bad Mom zipped through the elephants' gate, which was momentarily unguarded.

So, now she was inside the castle, but what a disappointment that was! The Bad Mom had pictured large ballrooms with chandeliers on the ceilings and fancy tapestries on the walls. Instead, she found herself in a dusty, very long, dimly lit hall. The dust got into her nose and made her sneeze. On both sides of the hall, she saw dozens of doors of various sizes and colors, each with a nameplate.

The Bad Mom read the names, "Susie, John, Christopher, Marie."

She tried to open the first door, but it was locked. The second and third were locked, too. The Bad Mom tried every single door until her wrists hurt. When she had just about reached the end of the hall, she came upon a small wooden door. The nameplate on the door read "Bad Mom," and a rusty little key was in the lock.

"Here goes nothing," muttered the Bad Mom, who, after all those days in the woods, had developed a habit of talking to herself.

She turned the key in the lock, and the door opened, creaking and groaning. The Bad Mom poked her head through the opening and immediately found herself in a sticky mess of spiderwebs with dead flies clinging to her face. She wiped her eyes, blew her nose, and had a coughing fit.

"Yes," she thought. "Of course, this would be my door - spiderwebs and dust. More cleaning."

The door led to a spiral staircase that was even darker than the hallway. The staircase wound its way up so high that the Bad Mom could not see where it ended.

She climbed the stairs and arrived at the end of the staircase, where she found another wooden door. The Bad Mom opened it gingerly and peeked into the chamber behind it.

The room was brightly lit by a large window, so she was blinded at first, but soon her eyes adjusted to the light. She looked around and gasped. There was a giant red bird sitting near the window, almost filling the room. The creature was at least four times larger than the Bad Mom. She did not doubt for a moment that the bird could gobble her up in a few bites.

The bird, however, tilted its head to scrutinize the Bad Mom. It was a magnificent animal with shiny, crimson feathers and a large black crest on its head. It had the curved beak and the penetrating eyes of an eagle.

"Krah," screeched the bird. "Bad Mom, what do you want?"

The Bad Mom was too stunned to talk right away, but somewhere in her mind stirred a memory. She remembered her mother telling her bedtime stories of a giant red bird that could fulfill wishes. There was a catch, she knew; the bird never granted more than one wish, and few people ever met the Bird Krah.

The Bad Mom took a deep breath. There were many things she needed and wanted. Food, most of all, a safe place to sleep, warm clothes, a compass, and a map of the forest.

"I want to be able to fly," said the Bad Mom, surprised because she did not know where these words had come from.

"Krah," yelled the bird, shaking its enormous body, and then it was gone.

The Bad Mom was left alone in the tower room.

"I must have been dreaming," she said to herself. "Hunger and exhaustion can do that."

But just as she started to head back to the stairway, she noticed something red in her peripheral vision. She craned her neck and yelped in surprise. She had wings — two fully developed crimson wings attached to her shoulder blades. She willed the right wing to move and gave herself a feathery slap in the face.

For a good hour, the Bad Mom practiced moving these wings, but then it occurred to her that she still had to find a way out of this castle. Wings or no wings, she was sure she would not survive another encounter with the elephants. That left only one way to go – the window.

The tower room was two hundred feet above ground. She looked down, and the meadow below seemed very far.

"I can do that," she said to herself. "I will. If it kills me."

She climbed through the window and sat on the sill. Her heart raced in her chest. Her mouth was dry, and her hands trembled. She took a deep breath and pushed off. She fell. The wind rushed through her hair. The ground was coming up fast.

"Fly, wings, fly," she begged, and her fall turned into a graceful curve; she leveled off and ascended, her powerful wings beating the air.

"Two rounds around the castle, please," said the Bad Mom to her wings, and her wings did as they were told. The Bad Mom saw the lions and the elephants below. They looked tiny from this height. She admired the ornate flower beds around the castle and cringed at the sight of the terrible forest where the wolves were still howling.

Then she laughed in utter delight and said, "Now, wings, let's get us something to eat."

The Bad Mom flew over the forest and found a small town where she alighted in the village square. Nobody commented on her red wings because these magic wings were not visible to most people.

In the weeks that followed, the Bad Mom traveled all over the land. Thanks to her wings, she was unafraid. She found the world a marvelous place, with mysteries in every corner.

One day, her journey took her to a village famous for its lush gardens. When the Bad Mom alighted on the outskirts of the town, she noticed that something seemed wrong. The fields surrounding the village were brown, and the parched soil was cracked. There were no flowers, gardens, or anything lush about the town. A stench of death hung in the air. The Bad Mom saw a dead cat next to the road and several rat cadavers. The village was quiet except for the buzzing of flies.

"Hello," yelled the Bad Mom, but nobody answered.

She walked from door to door and finally found one house where an old, blind woman sat on her rocking chair, staring into nothingness. She was emaciated, and her lips were crusted with blood.

"Hello," said the Bad Mom.

"Who are you?" asked the blind woman.

The Bad Mom gave her some water from her bottle and half a sandwich from her backpack.

"What has happened here?" the Bad Mom wanted to know.

"It was the cursed Bird Krah," croaked the woman. "It came to us to grant us a wish. Oh, we were happy before it arrived. Our village was famous for its beautiful gardens. People came from far and near to see our amazing floral displays. But we wanted more. Our days were perfect except when it rained. So, we asked the Bird Krah to make the sun shine upon us all day and all night."

"And so, you created a draught?" asked the Bad Mom, incredulous that the Bird Krah would have agreed to such a foolish wish. "Why didn't you ask the Bird Krah to undo this wish?"

"We tried," said the old woman. "But the filthy bird must hate us. Nobody has seen it in months. We cannot find it, and the people have left the village to work in the city. I alone stayed, in case the bird came back. Curse you, Bird Krah."

The Bad Mom gave the old woman all her water and food and took her leave.

"I will try to find the Bird Krah, and if I find him, I will ask him to restore night and rain for you."

So, the Bad Mom took to the air, got herself some provisions, and then asked her wings to find the Bird Krah. Her wings set a course due North. For seven days and nights, the Bad Mom flew, not resting or sleeping. She flew until the air became bitterly cold. She flew over snow-covered ground and past trees whose branches glistened with thin sheets of ice. She crossed ragged mountain peaks; then she ascended, climbing higher and higher until, finally, her wings set her down on a rocky slope overlooking the valleys and crests.

At first, she did not understand why her wings had picked this particular spot, but then she saw a flash of light coming from a nearby mountain peak. The light was a reflection from a large, golden cage. The cage sat all the way on top of the mountain, and in it was a creature that seemed ready to die.

The Bad Mom almost did not recognize it. It was the Bird Krah, slumped in the cage, its head hanging low, its plumage dull, and its crest limp. Then, just as the Bad Mom was about to take to the air to have a closer look, she saw something else. There was a creature wrapped around the cage. It was brown and gray, blending in with the rocks, and it was at least ten times the size of the Bird Krah. The creature lifted its ugly head to sniff the air, and the Bad Mom saw it was a dragon.

Even with her limber red wings, the Bad Mom had no hope of winning a fight with a dragon. So, she waited, and after a few hours, the dragon stood up, stretched its gray wings, and took off in search of food.

The Bad Mom flew to the cage, looking around cautiously to make sure that the dragon was nowhere in sight.

"Bird Krah, Bird Krah," she called. "What are you doing in a cage?"

With great effort, the bird lifted its massive head and focused on the Bad Mom.

"And what are you doing in these mountains of ice, Bad Mom?" replied the bird.

"I have come to find you. There is a dry village that needs your help, but on second thought, it seems that you are the one who needs help first."

"No one can help me," sighed the Bird Krah and closed its eyes. "I am already half dead and soon will be gone. Go save yourself, Bad Mom."

"Nonsense," said the Bad Mom. "There is always a way."

The bird opened one weary eye, "Maybe, but I don't think so. You would have to fly to the end of the rainbow and find the golden pot that holds my power. If you bring it to me, I can free myself from this cage."

"OK," said the Bad Mom. "That doesn't sound so bad. What's the catch?"

"The catch is that you must not use the power contained in that pot. You can't even open the pot. If you do, I will die in this cage, and evil things will invade your world because you are not meant to handle such power."

"Stay alive," said the Bad Mom. "I will be back as soon as I can."

So, the Bad Mom crisscrossed the land in search of a rainbow, but every time she found one, it vanished before she could get to its end. She tried, and she tried. It seemed hopeless.

"There is always a way," she grumbled to herself, and then she had an idea. "Wings, I beg you, find the end of a rainbow for me."

The Bad Mom closed her eyes and let her wings do whatever they wanted. After just an hour in the air, her wings set her down gently on a meadow. And there, in front of her, was a sparkling pot of gold.

The Bad Mom picked it up. It was not as heavy as it looked. It was smooth and warm to the touch. She heard a soft voice coming from deep within the gold vessel.

"Open me, open me," whispered the voice. "You will be more powerful than all the kings of the world. You will rule in justice and fairness, and all will bow to you. Open me NOW."

The Bad Mom saw her reflection in the shiny surface of the pot. Her mirror image looked magnificent, with a halo of light above her head, her wings spread like a royal cape, and her face benevolent and wise.

"I could be the new Bird Krah," thought the Bad Mom. "I could deliver the dry village from its curse. The villagers would adore me. I could defeat the dragon and free the bird Krah."

She paused in her thoughts, then added, "Yeah, but not right away. First, I would fly across the land and right all the wrongs. There are so many wrongs in the world."

The Bad Mom's hand strayed towards the lid of the pot, but she pulled it back before it touched.

"No way," said the Bad Mom to herself. "I am just a Bad Mom who ran away from her kids because she was tired of cleaning, cooking, and sewing all day."

The Bad Mom cried. It was the first time she had shed tears since leaving home. She removed her jacket and wrapped up the pot to muffle its voice and hide its seductive, bright shine.

"Find the Bird Krah," said the Bad Mom to her wings. "Go fast, my wings, for I am afraid it does not have much time."

When the Bad Mom arrived at the golden cage, she found the Bird Krah barely alive.

"Bad Mom," whispered the bird. "Have you found what I sent you to get?"

"Yes, I have," said the Bad Mom.

"And have you not opened the pot and not used its power as I instructed you?"

"No, Bird Krah," said the Bad Mom. "I haven't."

She placed the pot within reach of the bird and turned around so she would not see its power. Then she heard a violent noise; something was crashing and breaking, and lightning illuminated the valleys and mountain peaks. A fierce wind tore at her wings and threw her to the ground. Thunder rolled in the clouds.

When the skies had calmed and the cold sun emerged, the Bad Mom turned around and saw the Bird Krah. It was splendid, with its eyes ablaze and its plumage aglow. In its claws, the bird held the dead dragon, and it was ripping at the dragon's throat with its beak.

"Are you OK?" asked the Bad Mom.

The bird was busy devouring the dragon, and the Bad Mom wondered if she would be the dessert.

The bird paused for a moment, wiping its bloody beak in the snow, and said, "Excuse my manners, Bad Mom. I have not eaten in months."

"I better get going," said the Bad Mom.

"Not yet," said the Bird Krah. "I owe you a wish."

"I thought you never granted more than one wish," objected the Bad Mom.

"That is true for everybody else," said the bird. "But you saved my life."

"Well, if that is so, could you remove the curse from the dry village, please?"

"I would do that anyway," said the bird. "Don't you have a wish for yourself?"

The Bad Mom hung her head and whispered, "I miss my kids - and my husband, too."

The bird Krah wrapped its right wing around the Bad Mom's shoulders and whispered into her ear, "Go to the dry village and wait there; your family will find you. And when they do, tell them that each of them needs to perform an act of bravery. If they do that, I will reward them with wings of their own."

"Really?!" exclaimed the Bad Mom.

"Most assuredly," said the bird, and the Bad Mom took to the sky with a song on her lips.

*"So, what happened to the dad and the kids?" asked Fanny.*

*"What do you think happened?"*

*"Hmm, I think the dad and the kids got fed up with the discount mom. Then the dad hired a private detective to find the Bad Mom and bring her back."*

*"Really?!"*

*"Yes, but the Bad Mom insisted that everybody had to do their share of the chores."*

*"That's just fair," Michael said.*

*"And everybody had to do something brave," Fanny explained. "Like the Bird Krah said, so the dad and the kids could get their wings too."*

*"Why would they want wings?"*

*"To fly away, of course," Fanny exclaimed. "I want wings."*

*"Well, then, you have to be brave."*

*"That's all?"*

*"And meet the Bird Krah."*

*****

*"Do you have a real body?" Fanny asked the next night. "Or are you kind of a hologram?"*

*"That depends," Michael said. "When I am around people, I tend to be pretty solid, but when I go to the Soul Space, I am more like a ghost."*

*"Do you eat?"*

*"I don't need food," the angel said. "But I enjoy it. Especially Grandma's apple cake."*

*"When you eat food, do you poop?"*

*"FANNY!"*

*Fanny pouted, "You said kids don't learn if they don't ask questions."*

*The angel groaned, "Yes, when I eat real food, I poop real poop. I also pee."*

*"What does angel poop look like?"*

*"How about I tell you a story about the mysteries of the universe?"*

*"I bet your poop is as black as your wings."*

*"Do you want to hear the story or not?"*

# Chapter Three

# The Multidimensional Boy

There once was a boy who did not get along with anybody, not with his teachers, not with the other kids at school, and not even with his godparents. The boy's mother had died when he was born, and nobody had seen his father for many years. So, the child lived with his godparents, who told him his father might return one day if only the boy behaved.

The youngster was angry and argued about everything. For example, one day, the teacher explained how the Earth was a giant globe.

"Nonsense," growled the boy, crossing his arms over his chest. "It is a flat dish with some mountains on top of it. Everybody can see that. And I read it on the internet, too."

Physics was his favorite subject because his father had been a physicist. Incidentally, both of his godparents were physics professors, too. They had met the boy's father at the university and had become friends.

But when the teacher said that light was both a wave and a stream of particles, the boy had a laughing fit. Physics, he insisted, was truth, not some mumbo-jumbo of impossibilities.

One day, when the boy was twelve, he was home alone. His godparents had left for a conference, and he had the house to himself for three days. He immediately got into the liquor cabinet, and when he had finished a whole bottle of sweet orange liqueur, he threw up and then fell asleep on the living room carpet.

He woke up with a start. He turned on the light and found that he was still in the living room, but something had changed. He saw only a very thin square shape where the liquor cabinet was supposed to be. He tried to walk toward the cabinet to have a closer look, but found that he could only walk sideways, not straight ahead. Something was wrong with his sight, too; all he could see was a thin slice of the room. The sofa was a large rectangle, the curtains were wavy lines, and his shoes on the floor were small ovals. Then he saw his reflection in the mirror and almost screamed. He still had his brown hair, freckles, and blue eyes, but he was as thin as a sheet of paper.

"I lost the third dimension!" the boy exclaimed. "I am a flatman."

The boy was right; he was completely two-dimensional, and worse, his whole world was two-dimensional. The boy could move side to side and up and down, but not forward or backward. He could see only thin cross-sections of the world. For a moment, he wondered how an infinitesimally thin slice of the world could have any color at all. Then, he shrugged, went back to bed, and hoped to wake up to find the world normal again.

But when morning came, the room remained two-dimensional, and all the objects in it were thin cross-sections. The boy walked sideways into the kitchen and poured himself a paper-thin glass of milk.

When he had finished his breakfast, the boy left his house, meaning to go to school. On the way there, he ran into another flat child.

"Hi," the boy said. "Did you change, too, overnight?"

"What do you mean 'change?'" the girl asked, puzzled.

"Want to walk with me?" the boy said. "I am a bit scared to cross the highway all by myself. This sideways walking is hard."

"Sideways?" the girl asked. "You are not making any sense."

The two very thin children walked together and soon reached a park.

"Look," the girl said. "A baby tree."

The boy saw only a few oval shapes floating in the air. He guessed that those were leaves.

"Baby tree?" the boy asked.

"It's how trees start," the girl said, then she pointed out what she called "an older tree."

The boy saw some oval shapes in the air, but there were also some thin, worm-like shapes connected to the ovals.

"Those are stems and twigs," the girl said.

"You mean, the leaves develop into stems?" the boy asked, incredulous. "How do you know?"

"When you stand still long enough, you can see the leaves change," the girl explained. "The leaves grow stems, the stems attach themselves to twigs, and so on."

"Wait," the boy said. "Trees do not sprout from leaves. They grow from seeds. We must be moving forward relative to the tree; that's why we see different cross-sections of the tree."

"What's forward?" the girl asked.

At that moment, the world became black, and then, the boy was back in his bedroom; the sofa was again a sofa, not just a rectangle. The curtains were billowing in a gentle breeze, and yes, right outside of his window was a large maple tree that had no intention of starting its existence as leaves.

"That was a silly dream," the boy said and fell asleep because it was still night.

He woke up with another start. It was morning. He looked around, hoping his living room would not be two-dimensional again. It was not, but something was strange. When he glanced at the liquor cabinet he had raided the day before, he could see the cabinet closed and locked, but at the same time, he saw it open and missing a bottle of orange liqueur. The empty bottle lay on the carpet where he had dropped it, but it was also full and in the liquor cabinet.

The boy felt quite dizzy. He stepped in front of a mirror that simultaneously showed many different mirror images. There was the reflection of the boy standing in front of the mirror, but also images of the boy as a paper cut-out and of the boy sleeping.

It was time to go to school. The boy didn't even bother making himself breakfast because the milk was concurrently in the jug and a cow's udder (YUCK!).

He left the house cautiously because all the objects were simultaneously in many places. He almost bumped into a bicycle because the bike was two hundred feet away and simultaneously right in his path. Then, he came to a big intersection where cars were zipping by at breakneck speed. There was something very dark and menacing about this street corner; the boy could not explain it. This fear had started after his father had left.

He stood on the sidewalk and wondered how he would ever cross this road when he saw a car wreck at the side of the highway. The car was both new and destroyed. There was a man behind the wheel, simultaneously dead and alive. One version of the man was crumpled over the steering wheel, blood trickling out of his mouth. Another version was smiling and humming to himself as he was driving along. The boy made a stifled scream when he recognized the man. It was his father.

"Dad!" the boy yelled and ran toward the wreck.

"Oh, hello, son," his father said. "I have been hoping you would find me in the fourth dimension."

"I don't understand," sobbed the boy while his father took him in his arms and gently stroked his hair.

"I died or will die; it's all the same," his father said, looking forlorn. "I had an accident."

"I missed you," the boy cried. "Please come back."

"Alas, I can't," the man said. "My life is confined to its assigned position in space-time. But you must know I love you and am watching over you."

"How can you be watching over me?" the boy asked. "If you are stuck in this wreck?"

"My physical form is stuck in the whole of my life, not just the moment of my death, but the spirit wanders."

The boy's father paused and smiled, "The place I like to visit most is when you had your one-year birthday party. You were such a cute tyke. I made you a giant chocolate birthday cake with a single candle on top. You tried to eat the candle, but then you got hold of some cake and shoveled it all towards your mouth. Most of it ended up on your face."

"Can I go to that place, too?"

"Eventually, you will. I sent you the dimensions, my son, so that you would understand."

"Why didn't they tell me that you died?" the boy cried. "I thought you had abandoned me."

"I am so sorry," the man said. "Your godparents are good people. They probably thought they were kind, lying to you, but false hope can be the cruelest thing in the world."

"I hate lies," the boy said.

"I know," the man said. "Truth is precious, but not everything is as your eyes tell you."

The boy became pensive, "The neighbor's girl thought that trees grow from leaves."

"Yes," the man said. "Yes, she did because that's what her eyes tell her, but you and I know that trees grow from seeds."

The man paused. "And lives don't start from birth."

"What do you mean?" the boy asked.

"You will find this out later."

"Is light really a wave and a stream of particles, all at the same time?" the boy asked.

"It is, and once you understand the dimensions, this is not a contradiction."

"I am going to be a physicist, like you, Dad," said the boy, hugging his father, being careful not to touch the part that was all bloodied up.

"I love you," his father said with a warm smile. "I am so proud of you. I think you will make a remarkable scientist."

The boy woke up on the living room carpet again. The fourth dimension was gone, and the house was a mess. The boy sighed and picked up the empty bottle of orange liquor. Then he knelt next to his vomit from the night before and wiped down the carpet. It was time to clean up.

*"Did the boy ever see his father again?" Fanny asked.*

*"Yes, I am pretty sure he did," the Angel of Death said. "The boy became a famous physicist and developed ways to experience the higher dimensions. I think he and his father have coffee every second Tuesday in an interdimensional cafe."*

*******

*The next night, Fanny wanted to hear Hansel and Gretel.*

*"I have read that fairy tale to you at least five times," the angel objected. "Aren't you getting tired of it?"*

*"Not that Hansel and Gretel," Fanny said. "You told me once that you know a different version of it."*

*"Oh, okay," said the angel.*

# Chapter Four

# Hansel and Gretel

When a witch is in the house, it can be difficult to breathe. The air is heavy. The house is always dark. The children who live in the house with the witch walk on tiptoes all the time, but it is of no use. Sooner or later, she will get them.

Hansel was crying; it was Halloween, and he hated his costume. Hansel wanted to be Captain Hook, but Stepmom had gotten him a Tinkerbell outfit. To be fair, Hansel's costume was quite fancy. It had gauzy wings that shimmered in the ceiling lights and a glittery little wand with a gold star on top. He wore tight-fitting, velvety leotards and a sparkly pink top.

Gretel, on the other hand, had to buy her own costume. Well, she was pretty sure that her father would never miss the twenty-dollar note that she had swiped from his wallet. Gretel wanted to be a warlord, so she bought a gray wig, a black wizard's hat, and a fake beard. She found a night-blue, silky shawl in Stepmother's closet and glued some glittery stars to it. Now, the shawl was a perfect wizard's cape. Luckily, Stepmom did not recognize her shawl with all the stars on it.

Gretel felt powerful and wise in her costume, so she took pity on her six-year-old brother, who was still bawling. She went to her room and found her blonde wig from last Halloween.

"Here," she said, plopping the wig on her brother's short hair. "Now you look adorable. People will swoon over you, and we will get a ton of loot."

The thought of a ton of loot mollified Hansel. He grabbed his bag and flashlight and marched into the night, Gretel closely behind him. Gretel insisted that they should try a new, fancy neighborhood. They had to take two streetcars to get there.

"How will we find our way home?" Hansel asked, suddenly fearful.

"Not to worry," said Gretel. "My cell phone has GPS."

Hansel frowned dubiously. Then he looked around the front yard and picked up handfuls of shiny white pebbles from the family's decorative stone garden.

"Pebbles?" asked Gretel.

"Old-fashioned GPS," responded Hansel. "I don't trust you and your cell phone."

This was Gretel's third cell phone, and their father had threatened to kill her if she lost this one, too. But it had been two months, and Gretel still had it.

The siblings had not yet covered five houses when Gretel saw her friends and made a beeline to join them. Those friends were a gang of six teenagers, some with pierced lips and tattoos on their knuckles. Gretel immediately got into smooching her latest boyfriend.

"What's your little brother supposed to be?" asked one of the boys.

"Oh, Stepmom said it's gender mix-up day, so he is a fairy," snickered Gretel.

Roaring laughter ensued. Hansel looked as if he had just swallowed a lemon. The group marched on, with Hansel trailing behind, dropping pebbles. Hansel marked every intersection to indicate which way to turn.

Before long, the kids made it to the spookiest house in the neighborhood. The house looked old and decrepit, with peeling paint and boarded-up windows. A black wrought-iron fence enclosed the front yard. It was decorated with white, miniature skulls on each spike. A giant stuffed spider clung to the gate.

Everybody fell silent. There were rumors.

"They say this house belongs to a REAL witch," said Gretel's boyfriend.

"I have heard that she was in court for eating small children," said another boy. "But they couldn't prove anything, so she walked."

"She also has the best candy," said Gretel.

Gretel took Hansel aside and whispered that he could be a brave scout. So, Hansel puffed up his chest and opened the creaky black gate. He advanced toward the cobweb-covered door, waving his magic wand like a sword. He knocked, and immediately, a bony hand pulled him inside.

"Oh shit!' exclaimed Gretel. "My idiot brother is going to get hurt."

She ran to the door, and before you knew it, the bony hand pulled her in, too. Then, the door slammed shut.

The two siblings stood stunned. They found themselves in a living room decorated with skeletons, ghosts, and zombies. The room was dimly illuminated by a small lamp with an orange lampshade. Somebody had drawn a skull on the lampshade. Hansel touched the drawing and got his hand covered with something sticky.

The owner of the bony hand was nowhere to be seen. Gretel thought she heard a cackling noise from another room.

"Let's get out of here," whispered Gretel.

Hansel pulled at the front door with all his might, but it would not budge. Gretel yelled for her friends, but there was no reply. Then, there was that cackling laughter again.

"Let's see if we can find another exit," whispered Gretel.

"And some candy," said Hansel.

The children tiptoed through the house, going from room to spooky room. Gretel almost tripped over a black cat who hissed at her and swiped at her leg.

After a few minutes, they found the kitchen. On the kitchen table, there was a large bowl of candy. A sign next to the bowl said, "Happy Halloween!"

Hansel stuffed his pockets. This was high-quality candy, chocolate bars with almonds and coconut.

But then Gretel noticed an oven in a corner of the kitchen. It was glowing a fearsome orange and roaring with heat.

Gretel screamed. "She is going to bake us!"

"Nonsense," said Hänsel.

He pulled Gretel towards the back door, which was slightly ajar, and the children stepped out into the night. The gang, of course, had evaporated.

"Cowards!" grumbled Hänsel.

"I can't find my cell phone," wailed Gretel.

"Not to worry," said Hänsel. "We'll follow my pebbles."

Of course, there was hell to pay when they returned home, and Gretel had to confess that she had lost her cell phone. Stepmom grounded her for two weeks.

A month later, Gretel ran away from home. Hansel cried and kept the blonde wig under his pillow.

*"And the moral of the story?" Fanny asked.*

*"Moral?"*

*"Yeah, aren't fairy tales supposed to teach you something?"*

*The Angel of Death looked clueless.*

*"Maybe," he ventured, "It's this: When there's a witch in the house, siblings need to stick together."*

*"Poor Hansel."*

*******

*The next night, the angel wore a bright smile.*

*"I know a fairy tale with a very obvious moral."*

*"Really? Not something like 'burn the witch before she bakes you?'"*

*"No, it's about a young girl and her fairy godmother."*

# Chapter Five

# Veritas

Once upon a time, a baby girl was born to a man and his wife. The parents had longed for a child for many years, and when their wish came true, they were overjoyed. They named the child "Veritas," which means "truth," because the parents valued this quality above all else in the world. Every day, they prayed to their God to open their eyes to the truth, which they knew was divine and sublime.

Alas, as the years passed, the child became so ugly that even her parents could not bear to look at her. They locked her away in a basement room where only a blind maid was allowed to enter. The servant brought food and fresh clothes, but she never spoke a word to the child.

Veritas cried on her pillow for many months. One day, as she was all worn out from sobbing, and her pillow was soaked through with tears and snot, a bright light appeared in her room.

"Hello," said the light as it grew into the shape of a young woman dressed in radiant white.

The woman's face was as fair as alabaster, her lips were rose-red, and her eyes as blue as a tranquil summer lake. A golden tiara adorned her long, blonde curls.

"I am your fairy godmother," said the lady. "I have heard your cries, but, unfortunately, I cannot lift your curse."

"Curse?" asked the child. "What curse?"

"The curse of your countenance," replied the fairy. "It is so hideous that few can endure it."

The little girl did not know big words. "What's countenance? And what's hideous?"

The fairy did not answer, and Veritas started to sob again, "I just want to leave this room and get out into the world."

"If people see you, they will hate and fear you," cautioned the fairy. "Your face shows them all they don't want to know."

"Maybe, if I were invisible?" suggested the girl.

"That I can arrange," said the fairy. "But I doubt that you will be less lonely that way."

So, the fairy gave Veritas a veil that made her invisible. The veil was made of a shimmering fabric as thin as mist, and when Veritas put it over her head, she completely disappeared from view.

The next day, the girl stole the keys to her room from the maid's pocket and snuck out when no one was looking. She walked to the market, which was crowded with women and men. Nobody saw Veritas, nobody noticed her shadow. She heard the big and small secrets that people have and learned their hidden longings and fears.

The child remained lonely, though, and soon the sobbing started anew. One evening, the light appeared in her room again and grew into the dazzling shape of the fairy, whose dress was as blue as the sky on a sunny day.

"Child," said the fairy. "Didn't I warn you about this?"

"Is there no way to help me?" cried the child. "I am so lonely."

"Well, maybe there are one or two ways. The first is so abhorrent that I don't want to tell you about it, and the second holds grave danger for you."

"Tell me about the second one, then," said the girl.

"You can break the curse if you find a human being who can look at your face and not run away in fear. Unfortunately, you have only three chances, and if you use them all up and don't find a soul to lift your curse, you will die."

So, the girl started to search for people with good hearts and open minds. She wore her veil wherever she went but had whispered conversations with people as they fell asleep, so that they thought of her voice as a dream.

Soon, she found a young man who was a knight in the King's army; he had fought dragons, warlords, and trolls. When she asked him if he would help a maid escape from her curse, he agreed and swore on his knight's honor that he would not be afraid. But when Veritas lifted her veil, the young knight stared into an abyss so deep and so dark that it crushed his soul. He saw the nothingness of existence and knew that all his valiant deeds were for naught. He trembled and cried, then he turned from the girl and ran.

Veritas continued her search. The second person she chose was a woman who spent all day on her knees, praying and praising the Lord. She had given birth to twelve children and lost them all to the plague, yet she never abandoned her faith. When the girl explained that she had been cursed and only a soul without fear could redeem her, the woman gladly agreed. But when Veritas lifted her veil, the woman looked at an empty universe that held no trace of her children's souls. She cried out to her God, and only darkness answered her call. The woman screamed in fear and ran.

Years went by. The girl had given up on breaking her curse and made herself a home outside of the village. She lived in a hut by an old gnarly oak. The tree had been there for hundreds of years. It was covered with moss, and lichen hung from its branches like the beards of old men. Its roots went deep into the ground, and its canopy was home to squirrels and birds.

But then, as life will, Veritas met a certain young man. The lad spent his days studying at the library, earnestly searching for the ultimate truth. He loved philosophy and logic, the secrets of the natural sciences, and the pure beauty of mathematics.

Veritas, too, was fond of the library. She spent hours there, reading everything she could get her hands on. When she spotted the young man, she could not resist looking over his shoulder. He had a tome of mathematics open in front of him, and the table was covered with scribbled equations.

Veritas took a pen and crossed out one part where she saw a mistake.

The boy looked around, confused, seeing nobody. He tried to focus on his equations. Soon, an unseen hand took hold of his hand and guided his writing.

"Who are you?" he asked.

"My name is Veritas," said the girl. "I make myself invisible because my face is too terrifying to behold. If I were to reveal my face and the other person ran away from me in fear, I would die."

For many months, the two young people studied together in the library. The boy was charmed by this mysterious lady whose touch was so soft and whose words were so wise. He begged her to show him her face. The girl's heart was tender, so she agreed and asked him to meet her under the oak.

When Veritas arrived at the tree, a dim glow appeared in the meadow and grew into her fairy godmother. The fairy wore red gloves of the softest baby-skin leather and a long, scarlet gown. She held a gleaming, sharp knife in her hand.

"Here is the other way to break the curse," said the fairy. "If this young man fails you, like the other two have, you must kill him with this knife. Thus, you will save your life and become beautiful to behold."

Veritas took the knife and sat down in the shade of the tree to wait for her beloved. He arrived with a bouquet of roses and knelt before the big oak, where he knew his true love would appear. The girl's invisible hand reached for his, and then she removed her veil. Seeing her face, the young man blanched. He screamed and wanted to run, but his legs refused to obey.

Veritas regarded the trembling youth for some time; then she gave her love a gentle kiss on his lips.

"Live well," she said as she sank the fairy's knife deep into her own chest and died.

When the great oak saw Veritas's lifeless body, it groaned in dismay because it had always adored the girl. It heaved, and it creaked, and with one long shudder of its trunk, it absorbed her body and soul and every last drop of her blood on the ground.

The young man looked on in horror as Veritas died and every trace of her vanished in front of his eyes. He walked back to his village but could not find rest. His heart was full of guilt and regret, so he left his home and wandered the world.

Day and night, he remembered the girl's terrifying face. It danced in front of his eyes, holding a darkness so vast that he could not avert his gaze. He forced himself to examine his memory of the abyss, and slowly, over the course of many months, his fear began to fade.

Seven years passed, and the young man's travels brought him back to the old oak tree. He knelt in its shade and whispered a plea for forgiveness. When there was no answer, the young man's eyes overflowed with tears. Where his tears touched the grass, a thin fog rose, which took the shape of a young woman. She was wearing a veil, so he could not see her face, but the rest of her body, naked as on the day of her birth, was in plain view. The young man tried to touch the woman's arm, but there was no substance to the apparition.

"Please forgive me," sobbed the young man. "For I failed you and broke my promise to you. Is there no way to bring you back to the living?"

At that moment, a faint light appeared under the tree. It coalesced into the woman's fairy godmother, who was dressed all in black.

"I am the fairy godmother of this unfortunate girl whom you betrayed with your cowardice," she said. "You can still undo what you have done by using her knife on yourself."

The fairy pointed to a spot on the grass, and the young man saw the knife, still as gleaming and sharp as on the day the girl had plunged it into her heart. He removed his shirt, picked up the knife, and placed its tip against his bare chest.

"No," cried Veritas. "Don't kill yourself. All that's required is one drop of your blood."

With trembling hands, the young man nicked the skin over his heart. A single drop of blood formed on the wound and fell to the ground. Where it touched the grass, a red fog rose and mingled with the white mist that had sprung from his tears. Slowly, the young woman before him became solid and warm.

"Now remove my veil," said the young woman.

The man grasped the edge of the shimmering veil and pulled it from Veritas' face. What he saw was so terrible that it took his breath away. His heart stopped, his hands curled into fists, and a stifled scream tore itself from his throat. But even though he was petrified, the young man forced himself to look into the void.

As he did, his heart resumed its beating; his breath returned in ragged gasps, and his fists unclenched. He peered deeply into an empty space where demons howled about the futility of hope, yet he refused to avert his eyes. Then he saw stars in the distance. The stars grew and began a dance more complex than any mathematics he knew. They were glowing in colors of many shades, whirling around each other, and the young man heard the Symphony of the Spheres.

He embraced Veritas' naked body and held onto her like a drowning man. As his sweat mingled with hers, the abyss that was her face disappeared. A young woman's face formed before the boy's eyes, and it was gentle and kind.

The young man picked up the veil he had dropped on the ground and draped it over their heads.

Under the veil, he kissed his love's ruby-red lips and whispered, "Veritas, will you be my wife?" and Veritas nodded and smiled.

*"I don't get the moral," Fanny said.*

*"Not yet," the angel said.*

*******

*"Do you know any mermaid stories?" Fanny asked the next night.*

*"Two, actually," Michael said. "But they are both kind of sad. Unless you want to hear the Disney version?"*

*"No, I have seen that one on TV. Tell me one that nobody else has heard yet."*

# Chapter Six

# The Lellek

Morgan crouched in the sand, looking closely at an unusual seaweed. It was a fleshy, gray-green plant, smooth with a metallic sheen. It was about five inches tall and had bulbous parts on the top and bottom. The top was indented, making the plant resemble a spoon.

"This is a Lellek," her mother said. "It's very rare. Some people believe that it has magical properties."

"Can I have it?" asked Morgan. "I could use some magic."

Nina, Morgan's mother, hesitated, but then she shrugged and said, "Sure."

Morgan had been ten when she came down with cancer. It was leukemia, a nasty, aggressive version of it. Mother and daughter endured two years of medical torment: blood draws, bone marrow biopsies, radiation, and then chemo. The chemo was the worst part of it. Morgan clutched her mother's arm when the poison dripped into her veins, and Nina squeezed her daughter's hand as if she could squeeze the cancer away. Nina held Morgan when she threw up after the chemo. She spoon-fed chicken broth to her daughter while she watched Morgan shrivel away.

Two years of treatments, and yesterday, in the doctor's office, they had told Nina that the cancer was back and there was nothing more they could do. So, Nina rented the beach cottage for Morgan's last days because Morgan loved the sea.

Morgan pulled the Lellek out of the sand and attached it to her bathing suit like a carnation on a tuxedo. The Lellek leaked some greenish juice, which mingled with the sand still stuck on the Lellek root.

It was hot in the noon sun. Morgan stretched out on her beach blanket and closed her eyes for a moment, feeling drowsy.

"I bet it IS a magical plant," Morgan mumbled, already half asleep. "Do you think I should eat it?"

By now, the Lellek had stopped oozing sap, and it seemed to nestle comfortably over the bandaged port under Morgan's bathing suit strap.

"Let's not do that," Nina said. "But you can go for a little swim."

"Yes!" exclaimed Morgan, suddenly wide awake.

Morgan was a good swimmer. She had all kinds of certificates that would count towards getting a lifeguard job one day. That would never happen now.

Morgan waded into the sea. The ocean was calm and smelled of seaweed and salt. The water was so cold it had a bite. Morgan yelped when it reached her belly button, but soldiered on, determined to have a good swim.

She lowered her bald head into the water and dove into a breaststroke. The front crawl was faster, but she no longer had enough strength for this type of swimming.

The Lellek under her swimsuit strap seemed to take on a more vibrant hue in the green water. Morgan thought she heard it say something. She flipped over on her back to float so she could take a closer look at the plant. Where the spoon-shaped part of the plant had been, it now had a round face with two tiny eyes and a smiling red mouth. One of its eyes was winking at her.

"Hello, Morgan," the Lellek said with a watery voice. "Where do you think you are going?"

"No idea," Morgan replied. "Just somewhere I don't have to look at Mom's tortured face."

"She is taking it very hard," the Lellek remarked. "But I think she is wrong about one thing - a bit of my sap may do you some good."

"If you say so," Morgan said, still floating on her back and trying not to get too much water into her nose from the small waves that splashed over her face.

Morgan unfastened the Lellek and gently kissed its bottom end. The taste was bitter and salty.

"Urgh," Morgan said. "You taste awful. Couldn't you have warned me about this?"

"Ever heard of bitter medicine?" the Lellek asked.

Morgan shrugged, stuck the Lellek back under the swimsuit strap, and continued to swim. Strangely, her stroke seemed to be much more powerful than before, and her legs felt different. Morgan craned her neck to see what was going on with her legs and cried out with surprise.

Where her legs had been, she now had a fully developed fishtail. The tail was covered with glistening scales, most of them golden, with some red scales sprinkled in. The fin at the end of the tail was at least thirty inches wide, red as blood, and shaped like a whale's fin. Morgan moved it and splashed water in a tall arc of glittering drops.

"Lellek, was that your doing?" Morgan asked.

"Of course. And in case you haven't noticed yet, you can now breathe underwater."

"I am a mermaid!"

"For now," the Lellek said.

"Yee-ha," Morgan yelled and dove into the green water with a powerful thrust of her tail.

The thing about breathing underwater was that one had to inhale the water, which went against every instinct. Morgan held her breath as long as she could, until the urge became too strong. She gulped a lungful of seawater. The water was so cold that it burned, but the burning sensation lasted only a few seconds. Once the pain subsided, Morgan felt only a strange sense of peace.

"I should be drowning," Morgan thought. "My lungs are not gills."

Morgan touched her neck, and there, sure enough, she found her new gills. She ran her hand over them and counted six on each side. The gills felt soft and frilly and moved rhythmically under her fingers. Morgan dove deeper into the water until she could see the rocky bottom.

Suddenly fearful, she swam back to the surface, expelled the water from her lungs so that she could speak, and asked the Lellek, "Are there sharks in these waters?"

"Plenty," the Lellek said. "But they don't bother the merfolk. The mermen have sharp tridents, and the sharks know it."

Morgan looked around. The ocean stretched in all directions, still calm, with white crests on small waves. The sun was high in the sky, and the coast was nowhere in sight.

"Lellek," she said. "We are lost. Now what?"

"I can give you your legs back if you drink some more of my sap," the Lellek responded. "But I doubt that will help in this situation."

Morgan's stomach rumbled.

"I am hungry," she grumbled.

She could not remember the last time she had been hungry. Maybe that was a good sign. She wanted to tell her mother about it.

"Wait," Morgan said to herself. "When the sun starts to set, I will know where the West is, and if I swim East, I should hit our beach – or some beach – eventually."

The sun was still directly overhead, so this idea had to wait; in the meantime, Morgan could look for some food.

"Lellek, what do mermaids eat?"

"Fish and Lelleks," the plant said. "But please spare me. I haven't made any spores yet."

"I haven't had any babies either," said Morgan. "I always wanted a house full of kids."

A shadow fell over Morgan's face. It made her face look gray and her eyes sunken.

She took a deep breath, shook herself, and said, "OK, let's catch some fish."

Catching fish was easier said than done. Even finding a school of small fish seemed to take forever. The fish easily avoided her grasping hands, and Morgan resorted to herding them against a rock and then snapping at them with her teeth. After an hour of hunting, she finally surfaced with a tiny fish in her mouth.

"Please, don't eat me," the fish pleaded.

"I am hungry," Morgan growled, but she let the fish go because it was wrong to eat something that begged for its life.

The fish swam away and returned half an hour later with some of its friends. Between them, they carried a pink plastic object. It was a lunchbox, Morgan realized.

The fish dropped the lunchbox in Morgan's hands and swam away as fast as they could. Morgan opened the lunchbox, which held an apple, a sealed pack of cookies, and a slightly moldy peanut butter sandwich. Morgan devoured everything, snorting at the idea that mildew was known to cause cancer.

With her stomach pleasantly full, Morgan continued her exploration. Before long, the underwater scenery changed. She swam through a coral reef that burst with vibrant colors.  Morgan saw sea anemones, turtles, crabs, damselfish, and three or four inquisitive seahorses that approached her and then darted away.

"Hello," said a voice behind Morgan.

Morgan spun around and saw a mermaid with a silvery tail, green eyes, and long blonde hair. She seemed to be about Morgan's age.

"Blub," said Morgan, who had not yet mastered the art of talking underwater.

"You have to form a bubble in your mouth and then speak into the bubble, one syllable at a time."

Morgan tried and finally managed a bubbly, "Hel-lo."

"I am Amy," the other mermaid said. "And you?"

Morgan wanted to reply but found that her reservoir of bubbles was depleted, so she gestured to Amy to swim towards the surface, where it would be easier to speak.

"I am Morgan," Morgan said. "And I have only been a mermaid for an hour or two. The Lellek did it."

Morgan was about to point at the Lellek under her bathing suit strap, but the Lellek was gone.

"Oh no, how will I ever become human again?" she wailed.

"I fail to see why you would even want to be human," Amy said. "Humans pollute everything, and they can't swim worth a clamshell."

"My mother would miss me," Morgan said.

Amy thought about this for a moment, and then she nodded, "Yes, my mother, too, would cry if I disappeared. OK, I'll help you find another Lellek and get you home before dinner, but first, let's have some fun."

Amy and Morgan spent the rest of the day chasing each other until Morgan was out of breath, glowing with the exertion.

"This is the best day of my life," she exclaimed.

The sun descended towards the horizon, and Morgan said she had to go home. On the way, Amy wanted to know why Morgan had a bandage on her chest.

"I am ill," Morgan explained. "I don't have very long, I think."

"Mermaids never get ill," Amy said. "We die when it's our time, and when we die, we turn into foam."

"Yes," Morgan said, looking pensive. "I would like that. My death will be slow and painful, I fear."

Amy took the lead, swimming rapidly because night was near, and she wanted to be home before dark. Morgan followed as fast as she could, when suddenly, something hit her in the face. It was her Lellek.

"I am sorry I left you," the Lellek said. "I just wanted to look for a mating group, and then I couldn't locate you."

"It's OK, Lellek," Morgan said. "Amy is looking for Lelleks. Maybe she'll find you a mating group."

"Really? We are an endangered species. Lately, our mating habits have been out of sync."

The Lellek sighed, then he continued, "We bloom only when we grow as a large group on dry land, and our spores must be released all at once into the water at high tide. With the pollution of the oceans, we often don't get that right, so there are fewer and fewer of us."

When Morgan finally caught up with Amy, she found herself on a beach with hundreds of Lelleks, all in full bloom. They were growing close to the high-tide line. The head of every plant was covered with snowy flowers. Morgan planted her Lellek into the sand next to the other Lelleks and watched as it sprouted white blooms that swayed in the breeze.

When the ocean reached its high tide, all the Lelleks released a large cloud of spores simultaneously. The spores shimmered golden in the last of the sunlight and wafted over the water before they descended into the sea.

"I did it; I made spores, thank you," Morgan's Lellek said. "If you want your legs back, drink some more of my sap."

Morgan said goodbye to Amy and gently kissed the Lellek's head. The sap was sweet and smelled of anise. Suddenly, Morgan became very tired. She sank into a deep, dreamless sleep and woke up on the beach near their cottage. She scrambled to her feet and walked towards her mother, who was asleep on her beach towel.

"How was your swim?" Morgan's mother asked.

"Wonderful. How long was I gone?"

"Half an hour, maybe."

"I thought it was at least half a day," said Morgan. "I had the strangest adventure. The Lellek turned me into a mermaid; then I planted it on a beach with its friends so that it could bloom."

Morgan looked down at her swimsuit, and the Lellek was no longer under the strap. Of course, it wasn't there. It stood in its mating group near the water's edge and watched its offspring float away. The Lelleks would die that night, Morgan knew, and that was okay.

A few days later, back at the cottage, Morgan suddenly felt terribly weak. Her breath came out ragged just from walking a few steps.

"Am I dying?" Morgan rasped.

Nina suppressed a sob, then she whispered, "Yes, Morgan, the cancer is back, and there is nothing more to be done."

"I am sorry," Morgan said. "I am sorry for causing you so much grief."

"None of this is your fault," Nina said, choking. "And I cherish every moment I have with you."

Morgan was silent for a while, then said, "I want to go for one last swim. Please?"

"I think you are too weak for that, Morgan. It would not be safe."

"Mom, it's my time. I will be with my mermaid friends. Please, Mom, let me go."

Nina was silent, then she took her daughter into her arms and nodded, "Won't you need a Lellek?"

The next day, Nina went out to search for a Lellek. She combed the beaches, and when she finally found one, she brought it home and attached it to Morgan's swimsuit.

Mother and daughter walked down to the beach. Morgan was so weak that she had to rest and catch her breath every few steps.

When they arrived at the water's edge, Morgan kissed her mother and waded into the water. It was surprisingly warm.

*"Did she turn into a mermaid again?" sobbed Fanny.*

*"I guess we will never know," said Michael. "But her mother certainly thinks so."*

*"She does?"*

*"Yes, Morgan's mother often sits near the water's edge and watches the waves. And sometimes, when the sun is about to set, she may see a brief flash of a powerful golden tail with a large crimson fin that sends an arc of glittering drops in the air."*

*******

*The next night, Fanny wanted to hear a story about a monster.*

*"Sure," the angel said. "How about the story of the Worm of Disorder?"*

*"A worm isn't a monster," Fanny objected.*

*"This one was," said Michael and smiled. "It's what happens when you don't clean up your room."*

# Chapter Seven

# The Worm of Disorder

There once lived a man who loved to buy things, and he never wanted to part with any of his belongings, no matter how broken and useless they might be. By the time he turned fifty, his house was filled to the brim with his stuff.

One day, he came home with a box that held ten speakers, which he had found on sale. He could not remember where he had put the other fifteen speakers he owned. So, he put the box with the new speakers on the kitchen counter and forgot about them.

There was a stack of parcels on his porch, all full of things he had ordered online. Since there was no room for these boxes anywhere, he shoved them into the kitchen, unopened, and forgot about them, too. The boxes contained five identical T-shirts, seven pairs of sneakers, three bathrobes in different colors, fifteen can openers, a giant jar of ground pepper, toilet paper to last for a year, and twelve boxes of lens cleaning wipes.

Now, the kitchen was impassable, and that meant that the man could no longer cook. He did not want to spend money on restaurant food or delivery, but he had to eat. In desperation, he bought a camp stove with a little gas cylinder, two camp pots, some picnic plates, and silverware. He also got a box full of pasta and tomato sauce. He made room on his dining room table by throwing some of the various items on the table on the floor; then he cooked himself some spaghetti. He was very happy about his ingenuity and ordered six more of the camp stoves, twenty-four more of the gas cylinders, and a crate full of camping utensils.

When he had finished his dinner, he was tired and wanted to go to bed. His bedroom was on the second floor, but the stairs leading to the second floor were covered with heavy wooden boxes, crates, and bags. The man fought his way past the bags and crates, but when he reached the top, he lost his footing and crashed-landed on the hallway carpet, pinned down by seventeen heavy boxes.

The poor man yelled and yelled until a neighbor heard him and called an ambulance. The first responders used their axes to get through the locked front door, then they hacked and shoveled their way through the clutter and put the man on a stretcher.

The man had fractured his ankle and returned home the next day on crutches and with a cast on his left leg. He cursed and swore when he saw his front door, which was a mess of broken wood and splinters. He hobbled over to the neighbor who had called the ambulance, raged at him, and demanded money for the broken door. After five minutes of being yelled at, the neighbor withdrew into his house and closed the door softly behind him.

The man returned to his home and found that the front door was stuck on splinters and other debris. He put his full weight against it, and when he finally got it to open, he blanched. All the boxes, parcels, and bags that used to fill the hallway had disappeared. Instead, there was a giant worm-like creature on the carpet.

The man shrieked, but nobody came to help. The worm was about eight feet long and was covered with sickly white, flaking skin. The man thought he saw newsprint between the worm's flakes. The animal had six short stumps for legs and suction pads for feet. It was sleeping, so the man stepped around it and made his way into his kitchen. Much to his relief, his kitchen appeared untouched. All the boxes and bags were there, and the stove remained unreachable behind a wall of belongings.

"I am going to call an exterminator," the man muttered to himself. "But where is my phone?"

"I ate it," said a voice behind him.

The man spun around and saw that the worm was awake. The eyeless beast gave the man a wide, toothless smile.

"You ATE my phone?" sputtered the man. "Give it back."

The worm shrugged, which was no small feat considering that the worm had no shoulders.

The man remembered that he had at least three extra phones somewhere. He had bought the phones for an occasion just like this because he thought one needed to be prepared for all eventualities.

Then he had an inspiration. "I'll contact the exterminators by email."

"I ate your computers, too," said the worm with a voice as dry as its flaky skin. "All eight of them. Seven were broken, by the way."

The man screamed with rage and hobbled outside. He knocked on the neighbors' doors, asking to use their phones, but nobody answered. The man could see frightened eyes peeking out from behind curtains.

"The library!" said the man. "Yes, of course, I'll go to the library."

He flagged a taxi, grumbling about the astronomical fare, and went to the library. There, he found the contact information for a local exterminator, called from a library pay phone, and explained his predicament, crying and howling throughout his report.

"So, you have a giant worm in your hallway, and it is eating your computers?" asked the operator.

"Exactly," said the man. "Please send a crew over before it eats everything in my house."

"Certainly," said the operator, then he hung up without asking for the man's address.

After many more fruitless calls to all the exterminators in town, the man walked five miles back to his house.

"I'll be damned if I throw my hard-earned money in the maw of some greedy taxi driver," he muttered to himself.

Even with the crutches, the man's broken ankle hurt with every step he took. More than once, he had to sit down at the side of the road, wincing with pain. Finally, he made it to his house. The door was still splintered, and the worm was still there, and it had grown by a yard.

"Your kitchen was delicious," said the worm. "Especially the five hundred packs of ramen."

The worm had done a very good job. It had left some brand-new pots and pans on the stove, and there was a complete set of dishes, silverware, and utensils in one of the cabinets. The kitchen was sparkling, and the stove was easily accessible.

"Why are you doing this?" yelled the man, his face red with rage.

"I like to eat," said the beast. "I am the worm of disorder, and I am not going to stop until I have cleared every single room and the garage, too."

"Noooo!" yelled the man. "What you consider disorder is valuable to me. I can't let you have even one thing. Who knows when I might need it?"

"Need what?"

"Everything," sobbed the man.

Then he had an idea, "I won't let you eat my stuff. I'll eat it myself first."

The man limped into the dining room and started to gulp down some paper napkins. Those went down easily enough, so he swallowed a saltshaker, then a small container of ground pepper. He grimaced when the pepper went down hot as lava in his throat, but he still continued. Next was a bottle of ketchup, then a candlestick. Strangely, the more he ate, the larger his mouth and his throat became, and soon, he was able to swallow a whole camp stove.

"I would not do that," said the worm.

"Pfff," said the man and downed a camping gas cylinder.

The man's body changed while he was devouring his things. His legs became mere stubs on his rump, and his skin grew pale and flaky.

And then, BOOOOM, the gas canister in the man's stomach exploded, and all that was left of the man were splotches of blood and gore on every wall.

*"Oh no," said Fanny. "Why didn't he just let the worm clean up for him?"*

*"Fear," Michael said. "I think."*

*Michael paused, then he asked, "What scares you, Fanny?"*

*"Getting fat," Fanny mumbled. "The kids in school are really mean to the fat kids."*

*"But that's just plain stupid!" exclaimed Michael, frowning, all his feathers standing on end so that he looked like a pitch-black fluffball.*

*He continued, "Your body is composed of bones, muscles, organs, and, yes, fat. The composition of your body is neither good nor bad. It just is. And you have to get VERY fat before it affects your health or life expectancy."*

*"I am going to go on a diet," Fanny said.*

*Michael took a deep breath.*

*"Let me tell you a story," he said.*

# Chapter Eight

## Hair

Annie screamed while her mother labored over her hair. Elaine had handcuffed Annie to the kitchen chair and worked her way through Annie's scalp systematically, one strand of hair at a time.

"Can't we just cut it?" cried twelve-year-old Annie. "It hurts."

"You know better than that," said Elaine, frowning at her weeping daughter. "The hair has to be pulled out with its root so that it doesn't grow back too soon."

"Or shave it?" sobbed Annie.

"Razors cost a fortune," explained her mother, irritated because they had this discussion every time she did her daughter's hair. "Only the super-rich can afford razors, and since your father left us, we are just barely getting by. I may soon have to sell some of my diamonds."

Elaine had an immaculately polished, bald head decorated with surgically implanted diamonds, emeralds, and rubies. The gems were arranged in the shape of a rose, which was draped over Elaine's head so that the rose's petals kissed her eyebrows.

Elaine yanked out another strand of hair and put some ointment on the irritated skin.

Finally, after three hours of yanking and ripping, accompanied by Annie's blood-curdling howls, Eileen untied her daughter and said, "Enough for today. We'll do the rest tomorrow."

The kitchen floor was covered with a two-inch layer of hair, but Annie's head was only half done. The bald part of her scalp was angrily red and oozed blood. Annie sat down on the kitchen floor in a corner and cried. Her twin sister, Jeannie, crouched down in the pile of hair next to Annie and took her in her arms. Jeannie was luckier than Annie; her head was naturally bald and polished, and she only needed a few wisps removed every two months.

"One more day," Jeannie whispered. "One more day, and you will be done."

"Done for how long?" asked Annie, sobbing again.

Annie had been born with abundant, wiry hair that grew like weeds. Annie swore that the hair on her head wasn't just hair. It was a Hair Monster that sprouted back faster and more wiry after every pulling session. One day, Annie thought, it would devour the whole family, starting with Annie's mother.

Sure enough, a week after her pulling session, Annie had her full head of tight blonde curls again.

"We must be cursed," said Annie's mother while she retrieved the hand- and ankle-cuffs from the upper shelf.

"Please, Mom," pleaded Annie. "Can't we go to the doctor? I've heard there is a pill for too much hairiness."

"There is such a pill," said Annie's mother. "It's called Hairbegone, I believe. I think those pills are dangerous, though."

"Please, please, please," sobbed Anni. "I can't take it anymore. Nothing can be worse than pulling my hair out every week."

"I think that is a bad idea," muttered Elaine, but she picked up the phone and made an appointment.

At the doctor's, Annie and her mother sat in the waiting room, and Annie caught a few disapproving glances and whispers from the other patients.

Finally, the assistant waved Annie and her mother in, and the first thing the assistant did was measure and weigh Annie's hair. This required Annie to lie down in a specially designed chair with a hair scale attached.

"Your hair mass index is forty-three," said the assistant between clenched teeth. "That means you are morbidly hairbose."

After the exam, the doctor took Annie's mother aside and said, "This excess of hair is bad for Annie's health. It can cause cancer, heart attacks, loss of intelligence, and back pain. If you don't mind me asking, how did it get to this point?"

Annie's mother cried, "I try my best, but her hair grows back faster than I can pull it out. Don't you have a pill that would help?"

"Well, yes, there is Hairbegone," said the doctor. "It will make her hair fall out, but it will also cause her to throw up, bruise easily, and lose her sense of taste. She will be in a lot of pain every day."

"We'll take it," said Annie's mother. "The way she is, she will always be an outcast."

"You mean, 'How else am I going to find a rich husband,'" interjected Annie, then she grumbled, "I'll take the pill."

The new pill worked exactly as advertised. Annie's hair fell out and did not grow back for three months. Annie lost ten pounds since, to her, all the food tasted like cardboard. She did not go to school because she vomited every morning, her back hurt, her vision was blurry, and her face was so swollen that even her sister barely recognized her.

At the end of three months, Annie refused to take any more pills. The Hair Monster came back within a week, growing so fast and so out of control that it was like a lion's mane. Annie's mother went to fetch the handcuffs, but Annie would not have it. She kicked, bit, and wiggled until her mother gave up.

So, Annie went to school with this wild thing she called hair on her head, and none of the other kids wanted to sit next to her. The teacher never called on her, even though Annie knew all the answers. Her classmates tormented her with names such as "hairy beast," "Yeti," and "stink bug." The teacher gave a lecture about self-respect and self-discipline, all the while looking directly at Annie.

One day, during recess, there were screams in the schoolyard. The teacher came running and found one of the kids lying on the ground, twitching and spitting blood. The boy's head was covered with a thick mat of hair. The teacher sent the boy home, and it took his mother two weeks to get rid of the tangled mane.

"What happened?" asked Jeannie when she and Annie returned to the classroom.

Annie looked embarrassed, "I think it was my Hair Monster. Suddenly, the weight on my scalp was gone, and then there was a lot of yelling and crying, and then my Hair Monster was back on my head, and I swear it was laughing."

After that incident, none of the kids made fun of Annie again, and they all kept a respectful distance, hiding behind their textbooks, when Annie stepped into the classroom.

Meanwhile, Annie's sister, Jeannie, had her own problems. Even though her head was almost completely bald, Jeannie thought that what little hair she had was an ugly mess. She became obsessed with pulling out every last wisp of hair. She dug her fingernails into her scalp, hoping to extract hidden pieces of hair from under the skin. Soon, her head was bloody, inflamed, and covered with scabs, but Jeannie could not stop digging. She often ripped off some of the scabs while she slept. Jeannie demanded to go on Hairbegone, so her mother took her to the doctor.

"But your head is almost completely bald," said the doctor. "It's beautiful, except for the scabs."

"You are lying," cried Jeannie. "There are a million hairs. I am ugly."

"Wear gloves at night so that the scabs can heal," suggested the doctor.

Jeannie tried the gloves, but they did not help because Jeannie would take them off in her sleep.

One day, Jeannie stood in front of the mirror and cried at the sight of her oozing wounds.

"You may have a Hair Monster," Jeannie said to Annie, "But I have a Scab Monster."

The years passed. Annie and Jeannie grew up and moved into their own apartments. They were both miserable. When Annie and Jeannie walked through the streets, they found that they were as good as invisible to other people. They entered an ice cream shop and were the last to be served. They tried to ask a stranger for directions, but the stranger turned away, pretending that they did not exist.

One evening, they were visiting their aging mother.

Elaine greeted them with a radiant smile and sprang the news, "I am engaged, my sweet children. Engaged! My fiancé is well-to-do and dotes on me in every way."

Then, Elaine's face turned somber, and she whispered, "He wants to meet you, my daughters, but he can't see you like this. You both need to take Hairbegone. I have heard it gets rid of scabs, too.

"Hairbegone?" gasped Annie. "That stuff is pure poison!"

"No way!" exclaimed Jeannie. "You are out of your mind."

"Do it for me?" pleaded Elaine. "Also, my fiancé has two sons who are unmarried... See where I am going?"

"We are leaving," said Jeannie. "You can tell your fiancé that we both died in an accident."

The next morning, the twins walked by the town's harbor to look at ocean liners. At the pier, they saw a group of maybe fifty people marching up and down the quay, carrying posters and chanting. The protesters all had extremely long, messy hair.

"What are they chanting?" asked Annie, whose hair monster covered both of her ears with such a dense thatch that all sounds were muffled to her.

"I think 'Freedom for the hairy.' And 'hirsute is beautiful.'"

"Join us, join us," yelled a young man when he saw Annie.

The man had shoulder-length, red dreadlocks and a fuzzy beard that obscured half of his face.

"I am George," he said to Annie. "And you, young lady, are gorgeous."

Jeannie, whose head was bald and covered with scabs, looked down at her feet; her lips quivered as she whispered, "I can't grow hair. I was born without."

George scrutinized Jeannie, then fished in his pocket and retrieved a wig of long black hair, which he plopped on Jeannie's head.

"It's the intention that counts," he said. "Many of us have trouble growing our hair back after years of mistreatment."

That evening, George and his best friend, Peter, invited Jeannie and Annie to dinner in a restaurant by the name of "Hairie's." Peter was almost as hirsute as George. His blonde beard reached all the way down to his nipples. He wore his shirt half open to display his fuzz-covered chest. Peter's head was adorned with long curls, but there was a bald spot on his crown, which he tried to hide with a baseball cap.

"Did you ever wonder why our country has gotten to this obsession with baldness?" asked George.

"Sometimes I have wondered," said Jeannie. "In school, they tell us that baldness is the mark of civilization and hairiness is a return to barbarian times."

"Well," said Peter. "It seems it started with our late King Edward the Hairless. It is rumored that he was not a happy king."

"How so?"

"He was almost bald, and the three or four hairs on his cheeks could hardly be called a beard. In Edward's time, society frowned on baldness."

"Really?!" exclaimed Annie.

"Poor king," said Jeannie.

"Well, yes," Peter continued. "Every morning, the king looked in the mirror and screamed at his reflection. Finally, his advisers had enough of the king's constant howling and came up with a plan. It was an ingenious plan; they decided to make baldness fashionable.

"Soon, the images of bald girls appeared on the billboards next to the highways. Beauty contests were held all over the kingdom, and the winners were always the most hairless young women and men. After a few years, the kingdom became renowned for its hairless beauty."

Jeannie and Annie went home that evening, deeply in thought. The next day, the twins joined the protesters and, from then on, attended every demonstration, carrying posters that said things such as "Down with baldness" and chanting that hair was beautiful.

The four young people became regulars at Hairie's. One evening, George invited Annie over to his place. They had a beer or two, and George ran his hands through Annie's wild hair. Then he kissed her, and Annie let herself sink into George's hairy embrace.

Jeannie had a harder time. She was very worried about what Peter would say about the scabbed skin under her wig. She hesitated for weeks to see Peter alone, but one day, when the four young people walked along the pier, George and Annie fell behind, and Peter gave Jeannie a kiss.

"I know that your hair isn't growing well under your wig," he said. "Jeannie, I love you with or without hair."

So, Jeannie took off her wig to reveal a bald head covered with scratches and scabs.

"I think I see a small blonde fuzz," said George and placed his lips on her head.

"Nonsense," said Jeannie, but she smiled.

So, George became Annie's boyfriend, and Peter was Jeannie's.

"We should tell Mother about our boyfriends," said Annie.

"I don't know about that," replied Jeannie. "I don't think she can handle that much hair."

"We should give her one last chance," said Annie.

And so, the two girls stood in front of their mother's door, Annie with her hair monster that had grown into a three-foot-long mop of stringy blond hair, and Jeannie in her wig of smooth black hair that reached to her waist.

Elaine screamed when she saw her offspring, but then she waved them in, saying, "I have a surprise for you."

Elaine went to her bedroom to retrieve a brand-new, gleaming razor.

"It's a gift from my fiancé," she said. "This will solve all our problems."

"Not right now," said Jeanie. "Mother, we have boyfriends who love us the way we are. Would you like to meet them?"

"Boyfriends?" gasped Elaine. "Well, yes, bring them here."

When the day came, Elaine had prepared a fancy tea with crumpets. But when the doorbell rang, the first thing she saw was George. Then she saw Peter. Then, she fainted.

"I think you'd better leave," said Annie to George and Peter.

Elaine woke up screaming with rage.

"You dare to bring such uncouth barbarians into my refined home? You bring shame to your family. What have I ever done to deserve such abuse?"

Elaine yelled and howled, and then she lunged at Annie, trying to pull Annie's hair out all at once.

At that moment, the Hair Monster and the Scab Monster detached themselves from their respective scalps and jumped on Elaine. The Hair Monster had tiny, gleaming, red eyes and a toothy, wide mouth. It wrapped itself around Elaine's face. The Scab Monster had long fangs in its drooling snout and sharp claws on its paws. It leaped on Elaine's bald head and covered it with oozing sores.

The two girls looked on, wide-eyed and unable to move a limb. When, finally, the Scab Monster and the Hair Monster detached themselves from Elaine, they left a lifeless, bloody mess on the carpet.

"You murdered our mother!" exclaimed Jeannie.

The Scab Monster contemplated Jeannie and said, "She was very tasty."

"That was my MOTHER," cried Annie.

The Hair Monster shrugged and plopped onto the table to try some of the crumpets.

"I think we'd better go," said Jeannie, and taking her sister's hand, ran.

Once outside, the two girls looked at each other in disbelief. Gone was the mop of hair on Annie's head, and gone were the crusty, oozing scabs on Jeannie's head. Instead, both twins now had shoulder-length, wavy hair shining in the last rays of the sun.

The two girls left their mother's home behind and went to find George and Peter. The Hair Monster and the Scab Monster, however, started to haunt the homes of the bald, and now and then, they had a feast.

*"Are you saying if I go on a diet, I am going to get a Fat Monster?"*

*Michael scrutinized Fanny's face.*

*"Something like that," he said.*

*****

*The next night, Michael unfolded his wings slightly and placed a small pillow behind his shoulder blades; then, he nestled into the velvety red armchair. This was the only way he could sit in an armchair without crunching up his feathers.*

*"So, what kind of a story are you in the mood for tonight?" he asked.*

*Fanny pursed her lips and frowned, "Maybe a story with me in it?"*

*"Hmmm," said Michael. "You are not making this job exactly easy. Ok, how about this: 'Fanny and the Two-Headed Dragon?'"*

*"Am I slaying it?"*

# Chapter Nine

# Fanny and the Two-Headed Dragon

Fanny was bored. She wanted to go to the little village store one mile down the road, but Grandma wouldn't take her. Grandma was old and had creaky joints, and the long walk to town was too much for her asthmatic lungs.

So, when Grandma was taking a nap, Fanny took a twenty-dollar note from Grandma's purse and set out to go shopping in the village. She knew that Grandma needed aspirin, and she was low on coffee, too. The store also had a special kind of gooey candy that Fanny liked.

Fanny slipped out of the house and followed the mulched footpath. The sky was clear, the birds were singing overhead, and three or four rabbits were chasing each other in the mossy meadow. Fanny was wearing her flip-flops, jeans, and a pink baseball hat. She carried her backpack, stocked with cookies, an apple, and some water. The twenty-dollar note was safely tucked away in her jeans pocket.

Before long, Fanny reached a fork in the path. She thought Grandma had mentioned that one had to turn left at the first fork, but she wasn't sure which way was left or right.

*"That's easy!" exclaimed Fanny. "My left middle finger has a little brown spot. That's how I know left from right."*

*"Fine," said Michael, and continued.*

So, Fanny looked at her hands, found the middle finger with the brown spot, and turned in that direction. Unfortunately, she had remembered the wrong thing; she should have turned right. Fanny walked and walked, and by the time she realized that this was not the way to the village, the sun was dipping down towards the fields. Fanny was very tired by now. Her feet hurt from the flip-flops, and she was thirsty because she had used up all her water.

"Grandma!" cried Fanny. "I wanna go home."

Grandma did not hear her, but someone else did: A dragon swooped down from the sky and grabbed Fanny with its powerful talons. It had iridescent green scales, leathery wings, and a bright red crest on its back. The most remarkable thing about the dragon was that it had two heads. Both heads had sharp yellow beaks and forked tongues.

"Let me go!" Fanny yelled and tried to bite the claw that held her.

"Ouch," Head One said. "Keep doing that, and I'll drop you."

The ground was very far down, so Fanny resorted to begging, "Please, let me go, please, please."

"You are young and juicy," Head Two said. "Just what our three chicks need."

"Don't count your chicks before they hatch," Head One hissed. "You always jump the gun."

"Gun? What gun?" Head Two grumbled, then it turned to Fanny. "Do you see a gun? There aren't any guns here. My other head is losing her mind."

Before long, the dragon with Fanny in its claws arrived at a large nest that had been built in the crown of a sturdy old oak. In the nest were three eggs, sky-blue like robin eggs but five times as large.

The dragon gently set Fanny down between the eggs.

"The eggs haven't hatched yet," Head Two said. "You can keep them warm until they do."

"If I keep them warm, will you let me go?" Fanny asked.

"No way. You will be breakfast for the chicks when they hatch," Head Two said.

"They are not hatching," Head One remarked. "You dumbass can't even fertilize my eggs."

"Numbskull," Head Two snarled, "You don't know anything. Of course, they are fertilized."

The two heads got into such a vicious screeching and hissing match that Fanny put her hands over her ears.

"I am hungry," Head One said when they were done arguing, and the dragon took off in search of food.

Fanny was hungry, too. Luckily, her backpack was filled to the brim with Grandma's homemade cookies. The branch next to the nest had a hollow groove filled with rainwater, so Fanny drank and replenished her water bottle.

When the dragon returned, Head One carried an apple in its beak. It inspected the eggs, which showed no sign of life, and dropped the apple into the nest.

"For you," it said to Fanny. "You need food to maintain body heat and keep the eggs warm."

"One apple is not nearly enough," Fanny protested.

"I can get you a mouse?" Head Two suggested.

"Urgh, bring me a loaf of bread with some butter and cheese."

The dragon shrugged, took off, and returned an hour later with a loaf of bread, a stick of butter, and a thick slice of Gouda.

"Where did you get bread, butter, and cheese?" exclaimed Fanny.

"I know an old man who lives on the outskirts of the village."

"Mr. Miller?"

"Exactly. He always gives me food."

A week passed. Fanny kept the eggs warm and ate the food that the dragon provided for her. One day, it brought her an omelet; another day, it was a bowl of lentil soup; and on yet another day, the dragon provided a whole pizza with pineapple and chicken.

"My favorite!" exclaimed Fanny.

And then, one morning, when the dragon was out hunting, the smallest egg started to wiggle and jump. The shell cracked and out peeked a tiny dragon chick. It had black scales with an iridescent green sheen and a red crest on its head. It had only one head.

"Hungry," the chick squawked.

Fanny used her T-shirt to dry the wet chick and sheltered it under her jacket so that it was warm and protected. Then she fed it some cookies from her backpack and her last slice of pineapple pizza.

The days passed, and the other two eggs showed no sign of life. The dragon had been away for a long time now, and food was getting scarce. Fanny was getting worried that the two-headed dragon might have been in an accident.

"We need to leave the nest," Fanny told the chick. "Do you trust me?"

"Yes, Mommy," the chick said.

"I'll call you Drago if you don't mind," Fanny said.

Fanny put the chick in her backpack and began the long climb down the tree. Halfway down, Fanny lost her foothold on the rain-slicked bark. Luckily, another branch stopped her fall, and other than a sizable bruise on her butt, Fanny was unhurt. Fanny's hands were raw, and the ground was still far below, but she continued to descend slowly, one branch at a time.

When she finally reached the ground, she looked around and said, "Drago, I have no idea where I am. Or where home is."

The chick poked its face out of the backpack and pointed its beak West, saying, "This way."

"How do you know?" Fanny asked.

"I can smell your home," the chick said. "It smells just like your cookies."

"Fine," Fanny said and set out, hiking through the dense forest, climbing over tree trunks and boulders, and wading through a shallow stream. Halfway through the river, one of her flip-flops fell apart, and Fanny continued barefoot. And then, finally, she saw the village. She walked up to the village's only store, and there, leaning against the door frame, was Michael.

"What on Earth are you doing this far away from home?" Michael asked.

"I wanted to get coffee and aspirin for Grandma," said Fanny. "Is she very worried?"

"No, she is still sleeping. She is taking one of these naps, where you wake up on the couch at 2:00 AM, and you haven't even brushed your teeth."

"But I have been away for fourteen days. Grandma can't have slept that long," Fanny protested.

"It's been three hours," Michael said. "I have been looking for you everywhere. You must have been dreaming."

Fanny frowned, "If I have been dreaming, how do you explain my little dragon here?"

Fanny opened her backpack, and Michael peeked in.

"Cute chicken," he said. "Where did you find it?"

"It's a dragon," Fanny insisted. "I helped hatch it."

Then, Fanny had an epiphany. "You are tricking me, Michael. You are doing this time-thing of yours. You made it so it was two weeks for me and three hours for everyone else, admit it."

Michael smiled, blushed, and averted his gaze.

"Smart kid," he grumbled.

So, Fanny went into the store and bought aspirin, a bag of Grandma's favorite coffee, two packs of cookies for herself and the chick, and a new pair of flip-flops.

Fanny and Michael walked the rest of the way together and arrived home before dark.

Grandma was fast asleep on the couch, the TV blaring in the background. Fanny got a blanket from her own bed and spread it over Grandma.

"Good night, Grandma," she whispered. "Sweet dreams."

*"Did that really happen?" Fanny asked, her eyes wide.*

*Michael tilted his head and said nothing.*

*"Do we still have the dragon chick?"*

*"You mean Drago? Yes, of course."*

*Fanny jumped out of bed, put on her bathrobe, and raced outside. Michael extricated himself from his comfy armchair and followed Fanny to the chicken yard. It was dusk, so the chickens were getting ready to roost. Michael pointed to a pitch-black chicken whose feathers were scintillating in the last rays of the evening sun.*

*"That's not a dragon!"*

*"It's the one you brought home."*

*"It's a chicken."*

*"It's different from the real chickens. Check the nesting boxes."*

*Fanny opened the trapdoor over the nesting boxes, and there, nestled between a dozen white and brown eggs, was an egg, sky-blue like a robin egg but five times as large.*

*****

*The following night, Michael took his usual perch on the red armchair next to Fanny's bed and reached for the book of fairytales.*

*"Which story do you want to hear today?" asked Michael.*

*"No story yet," said Fanny. "I have a question. There are so many people, you can't possibly get to all of them."*

*"Time works differently where I come from. Earth will exist for seven billion years. I can rearrange all these days as needed. That way, I collect maybe two souls a day, and I can do a careful job."*

*"What happens if you DON'T collect a soul?"*

*"In the past, if I did not show up fast enough, the Red Snake would get the soul."*

*Michael shuddered. Earth had entrusted him with the souls of all human beings. Safeguarding those souls was his duty, his purpose, his sacred calling. He would never deviate from this holy mission, mostly because he couldn't. And he hated the Snake.*

*"The Red Snake?"*

*"Yeah, the Snake consumes souls. Souls provide it with its life force."*

*"Did you ever fight the Red Snake?"*

*"Indeed, I did," said the Angel of Death, leaning back and closing his eyes.*

# Chapter Ten

# The Fight with the Red Snake

There once was a rich merchant who lived in a fortified castle with a moat, a drawbridge, and all the luxuries a rich man could have. But the man grew old, as all humans do, and the older he got, the more he became terrified of dying. He consulted with all the magicians of the land and finally settled on warding his home against the Angel of Death. He had the conjurers apply three different spells against death. There was a spell that required a thin and uninterrupted line of salt and another that involved incense and long Latin incantations. A third spell was cast by a witch who boiled toads and poisonous mushrooms in her cauldron. The resulting nauseating fumes billowed in the man's kitchen. To make things worse, the old man had to hand the witch some of his poop, and that went into the cauldron, too.

*"Eeeouw," said Fanny.*

*"That's magic for you," said Michael and grinned.*

The old man was not content with just the spells because he did not trust the witch and the magicians very much. So, he also hired a learned man who painted ancient runes on every wall, window, and door.

The scholar assured him that Death would be unable to enter the castle, and the old man would be safe unless he ventured out.

When the man's time came, the Angel of Death appeared at the drawbridge.

*Grandma, who had been listening in, giggled. "Do you always talk about yourself in the third person, Michael?"*

*"It's a story, not a memoir," Michael grumbled, then continued.*

Michael looked at the runes and was dumbfounded. He wasn't entirely sure what would happen if he just entered the castle, ignoring the spells, but he did not want to take a risk. If the spells incapacitated him, the snake might get the soul.

To Michael, all souls were precious. Flawed or not, he wanted them safely in the Space for Souls. The Red Snake, on the other hand, would eat them, getting even fatter and redder in the process.

So, Michael circled the castle, looking for a way in, but found none. The protection by the spells and the runes was airtight. Finally, he took a seat on the branches of a giant old oak and watched the castle. Sooner or later, the merchant would have to leave his home.

While the angel perched in the oak, his old nemesis, the Red Snake, made its appearance. It slithered out from under some bushes and glanced with contempt at the angel in the tree. The snake was three times as long as a man. It was fat, and the scales on its back gleamed in bright, flaming red. The snake was enormous because it had been gorging on souls.

Michael felt burning hatred rise in his throat. The snake opened its jaws to hiss at Michael, showing two enormous yellow fangs. Michael thought he could see the little holes at the tip of each fang, from where the snake injected its poison.

The runes repelled the Red Snake, too, so it circled the castle and finally settled into the moat, where it waited impatiently. The angel could hear its angry hisses from time to time. Michael clenched and unclenched his fists but remained on his perch up in the tree.

Weeks passed, and the merchant stayed inside the castle. Finally, the castle door opened, but the person who stepped out on the drawbridge wasn't the merchant. It was the merchant's wife. She walked with a cane and was hunched over with old age. She wore a plaid robe and had her white hair in two braids.

She could not see or hear the Angel of Death, but she knew he was there, so she hollered and yelled, "Come here, Angel of Death, please. You are three months late, and nobody can take it anymore."

Michael stepped up to the door and dropped a note on the stairs.

It said, "If you want me to come in, you have to wipe off some of these runes."

"Yes, right away, oh Angel of Death," said the woman and ran to fetch a dozen oil-soaked rags.

The woman started to work on the runes, which did not dissolve easily. Some runes were painted with tar, others with the merchant's blood. They looked like stick figures drawn by a child.

The woman sweated and swore, getting tar and blood on her face, her hands, and her hair, until at last, she had removed all the runes from the door.

"Come in, Angel of Death," she pleaded. "Oh, please, come in."

She led the angel to the merchant's bedroom. The old man lay in his bed, eyes wide open, mumbling gibberish and wailing softly. From time to time, he swatted at non-existent flies in the air. The man reeked of decay. His hands were mostly bones, and his mouth was a gaping hole in his face.

"He has been like this for about three months," said the man's wife. "His body is falling apart, but the soul hangs on. It's unbearable."

The angel knelt at the man's bedside, grimacing because of the stench, and touched the man's forehead. The merchant's soul jumped into the angel's hands, quivering and emitting a sound like a screeching harpy. The color of the soul was mostly black, with only a few veins of light shining through the darkness of this soul.

The angel turned around to leave when he saw the Red Snake. It filled the doorway, its forked tongue flicking in and out of its mouth.

It fixed its yellow gaze on Michael and hissed, "That soul is mine. Hand it over."

"Absolutely not," said Michael. "I was here first."

The room's windows were still covered with runes, so Michael had no way out. The snake opened its jaws, exposed its yellow fangs, and hissed. Then it struck, but Michael evaded the blow with a quick dodge.

The snake, screeching and striking, pursued the angel, so Michael flew up to the ceiling and held on to the large chandelier. The snake could not reach him there but continued to try. It even crawled on the merchant's bed and over the man's decomposing body, but the angel remained out of reach.

"Go away," repeated Michael. "Go away, or I will kill you."

The snake laughed.

Michael deposited the merchant's soul in his shimmering carrying bag and attached the bag to the chandelier, out of reach of the snake.

"I warned you," said Michael as he nose-dived toward the snake. He landed on the snake's back and placed both of his hands on its head. The snake shuddered. The flaming red color seeped from its scales, leaving the snake's body dull brown. Michael jammed down his hands again and again, and with each thrust, the beast convulsed, shriveled, and faded.

It tried to buck off the Angel of Death, but Michael's seat was secure.

"You can't kill me," howled the snake. "You need permission from the Master of all."

"True, but I can reduce you to the size of a caterpillar and lock you up in a glass jar with some breathing holes in the lid," said Michael. "I'll be nice and give you some fragrant herbs for a bed, perhaps some peppermint leaves."

"I'll make you a deal," hissed the snake.

"What kind of a deal?"

"If you let me go, I will no longer take human souls except for those that are given to me willingly."

"Willingly?"

The snake tried again to shake off the Angel of Death and craned its neck to reach him with its fangs, but Michael sat tight and chuckled at the snake. He pressed his hands on the snake's head again, and the snake squealed in pain, shrinking some more.

"I will buy those souls from humans," cried the snake.

Michael grabbed the scales near the snake's head and squeezed them as hard as he could. The snake fainted. Michael blew his breath on the snake's face, and the snake woke up.

By now, the snake was only the size of a man, much thinner than it had been, and its body was a sickly yellow.

Michael let go of the snake and said, "It's a deal. Leave now before I change my mind."

The much-diminished snake slithered out of the room, and Michael, who had completely forgotten about the runes, retrieved his bag with the soul and flew out through the window.

"Oh, shoot!" he exclaimed as he crossed the windowsill. Then he noted that the runes had no effect whatsoever on him because the whole thing was just superstition.

# PART TWO: MICHAEL

*Tell me a story from when you were a baby," said Fanny. "Or were you ever a baby?"*

*"Of course, I was. I am told I was the cutest little cherub."*

*"Did you get into trouble?"*

*"Only a little. I learned how to fly earlier than all the other angels."* Michael paused. *"And I was Mother's favorite."*

*"Really!" exclaimed Fanny. "Did she bring you special presents?"*

*"She gave me my scary cloak."*

*"Some present," grumbled Fanny.*

# Chapter Eleven

# In the Beginning

Little Michael woke up in his crib and immediately started to cry. He was not hungry - angels don't need food - he just wanted his mother. Mother Earth smiled at her naked little cherub and picked him up in her dark arms, rocking him back and forth.

"Hush, little Michael," she sang. "I am here. I will always be there for you."

Michael put his thumb in his mouth and fell asleep in his mother's arms. When he awoke again, he pulled himself up in his crib and looked around. There were about two hundred cribs in the nursery. Each crib held a golden-haired baby angel with fluffy, white wings. Some were up and babbling with each other, but most were sleeping.

Michael fluttered his wings and noted that his feathers were neither white nor fluffy but raven-black and sleek. He flapped his wings as hard as he could and managed to get some lift. He crash-landed on the wooden floor next to his bed.

Michael got to his feet and walked to the nearest crib on wobbly legs. The golden-haired angel in it was awake and peered at Michael with curious eyes.

"Hi," said Michael. "I am Michael."

"I am Gabriel," said the other angel. "How did you get out of your crib?"

"I flew," said Michael, and fluttered his wings to demonstrate.

Gabriel tried to imitate him, flapping his wings as fast as he could, but did not take off.

"This way," said Michael, demonstrating a few slow, deliberate wing beats.

Gabriel frowned and concentrated.

"Ha," said Gabriel when he landed on the floor next to Michael. "That was not so hard."

The other angels watched these two, yawned, and went back to sleep. Flying was not yet on their minds. Gabriel and Michael, on the other hand, practiced their wings until they bumped their heads into the ceiling.

When the angels were seven days old, Mother Earth entered the nursery with an armful of white linen tunics. The babies had grown fast; they now could walk and fly, and they spoke to each other in the ancient language given to them.

Michael put on his white tunic and danced around in it, feeling all grown up because he was wearing clothes like his mother. He jumped about and flapped his wings until the other angels told him to cut it out.

Later that day, Earth announced a big meeting. The young angels assembled in the Great Audience Hall, a shadowy clearing framed by ancient, silver-barked trees. The angels stood silent, gazing at their mother. Michael had his thumb in his mouth and debated whether to run up to his mother and hug her knee but then decided against it. His brothers made such solemn faces that it seemed wrong to step out of line.

Earth appeared as a tall, dark woman clad in a flowing green robe. She wore a shawl made of the softest feathers of owls and held a staff of birch wood in her hand. Her white hair fell to her hips; her brown eyes were both kind and stern.

"Dear children," began Earth. "Today, you will learn why you were put into the world."

The angels nodded, their eyes wide with wonder. Earth's flora and fauna were all around them. Colorful birds cawed at each other in the canopy of mighty trees. A hawk circled overhead, and a fish jumped in a nearby stream. Small lizards scuttled through the tall grass, bumble bees buzzed in the blooming bushes, and a deer peered at the angels from behind a tree.

Earth continued, "You will be stewards for the most marvelous of all my species. It's a new ape called a human. Humans have what no other animal has: imagination, storytelling, and most importantly, souls."

The young angels hung on their mother's every word as she resumed her speech, "Souls are wonderful and mysterious. Even I, the Spirit of Earth, cannot create souls. The first soul appeared in a woman many thousands of years ago. She passed on slivers of her soul to her unborn children and also to the man she loved. The slivers grew into fully formed souls. By now, most women and men have souls.

"You, the Angels of Light, will serve to protect and refine the precious souls of the children of men.

"Now go, take residence in the town of Askalon, one Angel of Light to each human household. See if you can guide the people on the path toward virtue so that more light will enter their souls."

Then, Mother Earth whispered instructions into the minds of the Angels of Light.

"And my job?" asked Michael, removing his thumb from his mouth.

"You are the Angel of Death, and you will collect the souls when the bodies die," said Earth.

Something about Michael troubled the other angels. Michael was dark, he was different, and his very being was interwoven with death. They moved away from him until he stood alone.

"How does one collect a soul?" Michael wanted to know.

"You will be called to attend to a human, and you must touch them. Your touch will kill the body, and the soul will appear in your hands. I will teach you how to do this when the time comes."

Earth lifted her staff, and darkness fell upon the angels. When it dissipated, they found themselves in the hills overlooking the town of Askalon.

Gabriel, the leader of the Angels of Light, took Michael aside and said, "Stay back, Brother. The children of men shouldn't see you yet. You would frighten them."

"I don't understand," stuttered Michael. "And where is Mother?"

"If we want to lead the human apes towards the light, we have to get them to trust us," said Gabriel. "Mother told us that humans are scared of dying, so they must not see you yet."

Michael sat down among the prickly bushes and nodded, "Fine. But don't leave me here all alone for too long."

So, Michael stayed behind and watched as the Angels of Light took to the sky and descended in a well-ordered flying formation onto the town of Askalon. They flooded the village square with the brilliant glow emanating from their wings. Michael saw how the inhabitants of Askalon bowed and fell to their knees; then, the people led the angels into their houses.

"No way!" exclaimed Fanny. "They left you all alone in the hills?"

"No, no," said Michael. "Gabriel came for me later. Gabriel was my favorite brother. The others were always a bit scared of me, especially after they found out what my job would be. But not Gabriel. He looked out for me."

"Did you ever get into a fight with Gabriel?"

"Not really, well, maybe once. He tried to boss me around."

"And?"

"I just ignored him."

# Chapter Twelve

# Young Michael

At midnight, Gabriel came to tell Michael that he had found an abandoned shack where Michael could stay. He had put some blankets and a bed of straw in the shack.

"The people of Askalon are treating us as guests of honor," said Gabriel. "It is going well, so stay hidden for now."

Michael settled into his new home, waiting for his first call to collect a soul. Having nothing to do, he walked in the shadows of the village at night, peering through the candle-lit windows and wondering what humans were like.

Except for his black wings, Michael now resembled a nine-year-old boy. His step on the cobblestone pavement was light, and he easily melted out of sight when he chanced upon humans.

One evening, though, he was seen. Jeema was nine years old, cherry-eyed, black-haired, and olive-skinned. She wore a simple white dress and was barefoot.

"Hi," she said from behind Michael. "Who are you?"

Michael spun around and looked at the girl.

"Are you one of the angels?" asked Jeema. "You seem different."

"Kind of," said Michael. "I am supposed to stay hidden, so the people don't get scared."

"Scared of you?" snorted Jeema. "You can't be much older than I am."

"I am four."

"Four years? – You look older."

"Four weeks. We Angels grow faster than you human apes."

Jeema giggled, "Want to play marbles?"

"Marbles?"

Jeema taught Michael how to play marbles, and from that day on, the girl and the angel met every night, an hour before Jeema's bedtime, to play in the dirt.

Michael was unsure how his job of collecting souls would work, so he was careful not to touch Jeema. Jeema noticed that and put her arms around Michael's shoulders one day.

Michael shrank away and stuttered, "Jeema, no, I don't want to kill you."

"Do I look dead to you?" asked Jeema.

Then she demanded that Michael explain to her what his job was.

"I am the Angel of Death," explained Michael. "Or will be. I don't understand it yet. I think I will collect souls to keep them safe, but Mother has not yet made any of this clear to me."

"Mother?" asked Jeema.

"My mother is the Spirit of Earth."

"You are weird," said Jeema.

One day, Jeema brought a half-loaf of bread. It smelled delicious to Michael.

"Try some," said Jeema. "There is more where this came from."

"I have never eaten," said Michael. "Angels don't need food."

"Close your eyes and open your mouth," said Jeema, stuffing a piece of bread into Michael's mouth.

Michael's eyes widened.

"This is good. What else do you put in your mouth?"

"Sheep stew with peas is delicious, and I like figs and olives. I'll bring you some tomorrow."

Jeema crammed another bite of bread into Michael's mouth and put the rest of the loaf in his hands.

"I need to go, Michael," she laughed. "See you tomorrow."

That same night, when the moon was high, Earth appeared in Michael's shack. She had her long white hair in a single braid. She wore a suit of green moss and a cape made from butterfly wings. Her staff was fashioned from mahogany wood.

"Come," she said. "It's time you learned your trade."

She handed Michael a bag made from a gossamer, iridescent fabric.

"This carrying bag will guide you, and it will also keep the souls safe. Never let it out of your sight."

Michael slung the bag over his right shoulder and immediately felt a tug.

"Follow the tug," said Earth.

Before long, Michael and Earth stood at the deathbed of an old man. The man was gasping for air in his sleep.

"Put your hand on his face and ask the soul to come to you," said Earth.

Michael obeyed, and a translucent orb formed in his hands. The man became still. Michael shrank away from the corpse.

"Did I just kill that man?"

"Yes," replied Earth. "You are the Angel of Death. When you call the soul into your hands, the body dies."

Next, Earth put her arm around Michael's shoulder, and they ascended together high into the sky. Michel had never been this high up. The air was chilly and thin. Michel's breathing became labored.

"A little further," said Earth.

Michael's head started to spin, pearls of sweat formed on his forehead, and the stars in the night sky began a dizzying dance.

"I cannot go any higher," he gasped. "I can't breathe."

"Good," said Earth. "Now will yourself to a different place. It's a place of safety I made for the souls. I call it 'the Space for Souls.'"

Michael put the last bit of his fading mind into concentrating and felt a jolt. The scenery changed to a featureless, silent room in which he floated weightlessly. A soft light that had no apparent source permeated the space. Earth moved her staff, and a small alcove took shape.

"Put the soul there," said Earth. "It will sleep there for now."

"What will happen to the soul?"

"It is sleeping," repeated Earth.

"Yes, I know, but in the long run?"

"None of your business," said Earth. "Just do your job."

When Michael returned to the ordinary world, he began his job of collecting souls as ordered.

One day, on his way to a dying woman, he ran into a group of Angels of Light. Five or six of them were laughing and joking with each other. One looked Michael up and down and wrinkled his nose in disgust.

"Go away, Angel of Death," he said. "You smell of decay."

The group of angels turned around and walked away from Michael.

Michael examined his white tunic for smells and stains, but it seemed clean to him. After all, he washed it every night in the brook behind his shed and hung it up to dry on the olive tree that grew near it.

Even though he was busy with his death-angel duties, Michael had spare time to play with Jeema. One night, though, Jeema did not show up. Michael stood before her house, calling her name, but nobody answered.

Two days later, the tug of his carrying bag led him into Jeema's home. When Michael stepped into the main room, Jeema's mother hissed at him like a wild animal, and her father took out his knife. Jeema lay on her bed, choking and coughing, and her face was flushed. Michael explained to the parents that he was sent by orders of the Great Spirit of Earth, and they backed away from him.

Jeema recognized Michael even in her fever and whispered, "Get it over with, Michael, please."

Michael caressed Jeema's burning face, and her rattling breath subsided; then, her soul appeared in his hands. At that moment, Jeema's mother lunged at Michael, scratching his face. Jeema's father tried to put his hands around Michael's throat. Michael ducked and jumped through the window and into the sky.

Jeema's young soul was small; it had a soft glow and simple patterns in rose gold and green. Michael put the soul into his carrying bag and ascended to ten thousand feet, where he made the jump to the Space for Souls. He placed Jeema's soul on a soft cushion.

"Good night, Jeema," he whispered, but the soul did not respond.

When he returned to Askalon, there was an aching emptiness in his chest for which he had no name. After another month of collecting souls, Michael asked Gabriel to meet him on the beach.

"I am leaving, Gabriel," said Michael.

The two angels stood on a dune overlooking the Mediterranean Sea. Gabriel put his arm around Michael's shoulders and ruffled his black hair.

"I know that you hate your job, Brother. But it is Earth who gave it to you. You don't think you can defy our creator?"

Michael shook his head. "I want to plead with her."

Gabriel frowned. "Do you even know where to look for her?"

"The Great Audience Hall. It's where we last saw her."

"And how will you find the Audience Hall? We were transported here in the blink of an eye."

Michael pointed across the waters where the sun was setting.

"This way," Michael said. "I can feel her this way. It's a different kind of pull, not the tug that leads me to a dying person. It's Mother, I am sure."

"You want to go West?" asked Gabriel. "How far West?'

"I don't know. I will just fly until I get there."

"That's suicide, Michael!" exclaimed Gabriel. "Do you have any idea how big this water is? It could be a hundred miles across."

"I don't think we angels can die – not without Mother's permission," said Michael. "And if I die, won't I return into her arms?"

"You are insane," said Gabriel, puffing up his chest and trying to stare Michael down. "Michael, you will not leave. I forbid it."

"On what authority?"

"I am the leader of the angels, remember?"

"You are the leader of the Angels of Light, Gabriel. I stand alone; I answer only to the Spirit of Earth."

"Don't be stupid, Michael. Earth is bound to check up on us sooner or later. Just stay put."

"Goodbye, Gabriel," said Michael and took off, flying towards the setting sun.

"So what happened?" asked Fanny the next night. "Did you make it across the ocean?"

"Two oceans, actually," replied Michael. "Frankly, the whole thing was stupid of me. I was so young, and I had no idea what I was getting myself into."

"Well, you needed to see your mother. I would fly across oceans to find Grandma, too."

"Yes," Michael said, smiling. "Your Grandma is worth a flight across oceans."

# Chapter Thirteen

# The Flight Across Two Oceans

Michael flew without rest for five days and nights. He got as far as the Coast of Spain when a sudden storm barreled down on him. The gale pulled at his wings and tossed him around like a rag doll. Michael tried to ride it out by climbing above the black thunder clouds, but the wind grabbed him and threw him into the wild surf below.

"Mother!" cried Michael.

A giant wave swallowed him and pulled him under. Michael, his lungs full of seawater, drifted in the deep green, closed his eyes, and let the waves rock him. He stayed submerged until the storm above the sea calmed, then he swam to the surface and shook out his wings.

"Mother!" Michael cried again, expelling the seawater from his lungs, but there was no response.

The young angel took to the sky, flying again to the West. He crossed the densely forested land mass of Spain and then came upon the next enormous body of water, the Atlantic.

For three months, Michael fought with currents and gusts. When the wind was too rough, he rode it out by floating submerged under the waves. The sharks and the other big creatures of the sea left him alone.

Finally, a fog-covered coastline appeared on the horizon. Earth was near now; Michael could feel it. He found the mouth of a mighty stream and followed the muddy, wide river inland. The closer Michael got to his mother, the more varied and abundant nature became. The river below him carried thousands of species of fish. Ancient trees, covered with lichen and moss, were home to small, agile monkeys. The monkeys jumped from tree to tree, trying to keep up with Michael as he fought his way upstream. Colorful birds cawed, chirped, and sang to the young angel who continued to wing his way West.

At last, Michael arrived at the waterfall that hid the entrance to the Great Audience Hall.

Michael's face and arms were burned from months in the sun; he had lost half of his feathers, and his black hair was long and windswept. He was barefoot because the waters had stolen his sandals, and his white tunic was dirty and in tatters.

Michael walked up to the polished tree stump that marked the center of the Audience Hall and cried, "Mother Earth, please hear me. It's me, Michael."

When there was no answer, Michael curled up next to the tree stump, fluffed up the few feathers he had left against the cool air of the night, and fell asleep.

He woke up to a gentle touch on his shoulder.

"What are you doing here, my little Angel of Death?" asked Earth. "Did I not assign you enough work?"

"Oh, please, Mother, there is plenty of work, but I am not cut out to do it. Can't you give me another job?"

Earth's voice was gentle when she asked to hear more.

"A few days after you left me," said Michael. "I was called to collect a soul that belonged to a nine-year-old girl. Her name was Jeema. Such a sweet girl! She used to play marbles with me before she fell sick."

Michael paused for a moment, his lower lip quivering.

"Her parents tried to attack me when I came to collect her soul. I got away only because I have wings."

Earth nodded, "Humans tend to take the deaths of their young very hard. Yet, such is the circle of life."

"The next death happened two days later," continued Michael. "The village's chief was dying of wound fever. He was red-faced, evil-smelling, and covered with sweat. He mumbled incoherently to himself. The villagers waited for me outside the house. They were armed with clubs and spears. One woman brought a kettle full of boiling oil. I had to steal the soul under the cover of night, but the people almost caught me.

"It's like that every time I come for a soul. They all hate me. Even the other angels despise me – all except Gabriel, my only friend."

Earth took Michael in her arms and rocked him in her embrace.

"We'll have to make you more fearsome, little Angel of Death," she said. "Wear this."

Earth handed Michael a hooded black cloak. The cloak hung loose on the small angel, and its hood shrouded his face in deep shadows.

"Your face is too gentle," explained Earth. "Make sure that you keep your countenance hidden when you work. Also, I have imbued the cloak with powerful pheromones of fear. No human will dare attack you when you wear it."

"I don't want to kill," whispered Michael. "Maybe one of the other angels would be more suitable?"

"No, Michael, none of the other angels could handle this job. Do you think that any of them would have chanced the journey across two oceans? You are brave and tenacious. I picked you for a reason."

"I like humans. Please don't make me their killer."

"Don't be silly, Michael. When you are called to collect a soul, death is already upon the body. All you do is make it merciful and quick."

"What happens to the souls I collect?"

Earth sighed, "It's complicated, but I think you have earned yourself an answer.

"Good, light-filled souls sing wonderful songs. I want to create a grand music, the Symphony of the Spheres."

"And those souls who are not that perfect?"

"Once there are enough human beings, these souls can choose to be reborn. Thus, they will have a chance to improve their light."

"And in the end, when the symphony is done, and life on Earth is finished?"

"Then I will cease to exist," said Earth. "Nirvana, I think."

"I love you, Mother," said Michael.

"I love you, too, child of my heart. You are precious to me, even more so than all the souls."

Michael fell asleep in his mother's arms. While he slept, she blew her breath over his wings and face to restore his beauty and health. She then clothed him all in black and sent him back to Askalon, where he awoke in his shack. Michael went to work the next day wearing his cloak. The people blanched when they saw him enter a house, and no one tried to interfere.

*"There is more to the story, isn't there?" asked Fanny.*

*Michael sighed and said, "Yes, but I am not at all sure it's age appropriate."*

*Fanny pouted, so Michael shrugged and began.*

# Chapter Fourteen

# The Slaughter of the Angels

Michael was worried. Lately, something strange was happening to the souls he collected. It started one evening, when he stepped to the deathbed of the Major of Askalon and called for the man's soul. The Major, a white-haired man in his eighties, groaned and took his last shuddering breath.

When the angel looked at the soul in his hands, he winced. There was no light in that soul, none at all. The sphere was completely black with not even a little vein of brightness running through it. Its music was a low drone without any highs or lows. Before Michael could place the globe in his shimmering transport bag, it crumbled under his gaze. The sphere disintegrated into flakes of black soot, which dissolved into a small dark cloud of smoke, and then it was gone.

"This isn't right," Michael said, dumbfounded, because he could not do his job with souls this unstable.

When the same thing happened three more times in a span of only a week, Michael went to talk to Gabriel.

He found his brother sitting in an armchair on his porch overlooking the sea. The scent of seaweed and salt wafted in the air. Gabriel sipped from a glass of burgundy wine. A young slave girl stood behind her master's chair, fanning him with a large palm leaf. Another slave girl tiptoed into the room carrying a tray with delicacies, such as tongues of swallows and hearts of unborn lambs, which she offered to Gabriel and Michael. Her eyes were downcast, and she seemed fearful of both angels.

"Gabriel," Michael said. "Lately, some of the souls I am collecting from Askalon are brittle and dark as night. I can't even bring them to the Place for Souls. Aren't you Angels of Light supposed to increase the light in the souls under your care?"

Gabriel reassured Michael that the Angels of Light were doing all they could, but an occasional bad apple was to be expected.

In fact, Gabriel admitted, he had recently been summoned to appear before Earth, who had noticed the same thing. Gabriel had promised to increase his monthly sermons and preach the virtues to the inhabitants of Askalon.

"What virtues?" Micael asked.

"Moderation, first of all, and humility and mercy, of course."

"Are you practicing those?"

"That's for humans," Gabriel scoffed.

"Since when do you keep slaves?" Michael wanted to know.

"Aren't they gorgeous?" Gabriel replied, then he explained how he had come to be a slave owner:

Askalon had been under attack. The sounds of war cries and ram's horns flooded the village. Fierce, bearded men carrying bows, arrows, and spears poured into the village square. They set fire to the houses and stabbed to death men, women, and children.

When Gabriel saw the carnage, he summoned the Angels of Light under his command. They descended on the marauding horde, sending arrows down on the attackers. When all the hostile forces lay dead in the village square, the elders of Askalon gathered their surviving warriors and set out to loot the homes of the enemy. They returned to Askalon with treasure, cattle, and slaves.

"Gabriel, we are most grateful to you and our other guardian angels," said the elder, bowing before Gabriel. "Please, take your pick of the slaves."

"I don't think angels should keep slaves," Michael mused, but Gabriel shrugged, saying that the angels treated their slaves very well.

Michael took his leave and flew to the city that had attacked Askalon. He found only ruins, burnt-out houses, and rubble on every street. The few surviving inhabitants looked like ghosts, undernourished and furtive.

Next, Michael visited the marketplace of Askalon. Men, women, and children were milling about, all dressed in colorful clothes. The women wore jewelry of gold and sapphire, and the men's suits were made of the finest lamb's wool. There was a profusion of fruits and vegetables on the market stands, and chickens and goats were offered for slaughter. The roads were lush with greenery. Slaves in dirty rags swept the streets, watered, and raked the flower gardens. As Michael walked across the cobble-stoned plaza, he heard screams and the sounds of a whip.

A few days later, Michael went to visit Gabriel again. It was midnight. The town of Askalon was quiet, and all the angels were inside with their humans, one angel in each house.

Michael knocked at Gabriel's door, and Gabriel himself opened it for him. There was a curtain between the door and the living room, so Michael could not see what was happening behind it, but he had a pretty good idea anyway.

Gabriel was wearing a white tunic and leather sandals. He had a green wreath of olive leaves on his blonde head and a gold chain around his neck. His radiant white wings were neatly folded on his back.

"Yes?" said Gabriel.

A dark-skinned human girl poked through the curtain and screeched, "It's the Angel of Death! Gabriel, make him go away."

"Gabriel, please," said Michael. "We need to talk. I am not here to take any souls, just to talk."

Behind the curtain were more shrieks, laughter, and drunken singing.

"We are having fun," said Gabriel. "Why are you interrupting?"

"Because if you don't stop this insanity, it will not end well for you," said Michael.

At that moment, another human girl, who could not have been older than twelve, tumbled through the curtain holding a jug of wine. She was about to offer some to Michael when she noticed his black cloak and ran away screaming.

"Spoilsport," said Gabriel, and slammed the door in Michael's face.

Michael went from house to house, pleading with the resident angels, but to no avail. The villagers ran away scared when they saw his cloak and black wings, and the Angels of Light turned him away.

Michael took to the air and perched on a nearby hill that offered a good view of the village. He settled down with a heavy heart. Sure enough, with the early morning came thunder and lightning. The ground itself rumbled and shook. Then, Michael saw an enormous, crimson snake appear in a cloud of red dust and slither into the village. The snake went from house to house, pulling the angels away from their human hosts.

The angels were much too drunk to offer any resistance. The snake sank its fangs into their bodies, and when all of the Angels of Light lay dead in the village square, the snake had its feast. When it finally had its fill, it slithered away. It left dozens of wings and heads in the Cobblestone Square. The blood of the angels coated the benches and the village well.

The people of Askalon were hiding in their houses. None dared to show their faces, but they peered through their windows as Michael waded through the remains of the angels. At last, Michael found what was left of Gabriel, his only friend among the Angels of Light. Gabriel was only half eaten, his body contorted, and his eyes unseeing. Michael collected the remains of all the angels and buried them under a big olive tree. He would have cried but had not yet learned how to shed tears. He washed his bloodied hands in the well when he heard a summons. Earth herself demanded his presence, so Michael stood up to await the darkness that would transport him to the Audience Hall.

As before, Earth's Great Audience Hall was hidden in the midst of a jungle. Tall trees joined branches to form a majestic roof, creating a space as shadowy and holy as a cathedral. A large, polished tree stump formed a podium in the center of the audience hall. Small white flowers grew in profusion around the podium, and brilliantly colored birds sang in the canopy of the trees.

"Michael," echoed the invisible Presence of Earth, "You angels have gravely disappointed me. You were sent to guide and discipline the children of men. Instead, you have made yourselves into a bunch of depraved drunkards cavorting around with the daughters of men."

Michael stood silent before his master's wrath.

"Have you nothing to say on your own behalf?" bellowed Earth.

"My Master, I have not participated in feasts or drunkenness."

At that moment, the Red Snake slithered into the Audience Hall and hissed, "You did not participate because the children of men wouldn't have you. You are the bringer of death, so they shun you."

"And the bringer of death is all you will be," decreed Earth. "From now on, humans will know your presence only through a sense of unreasoned fear. They will not see you or hear you. Furthermore, your death touch will no longer be at your whim; you will bring death to any living being you touch, whether you wish it or not. That way, Michael, you will serve me and me alone."

Michael bowed his head in acknowledgment, but Earth was not done.

"The Red Snake will be allowed to devour what flawed souls it can catch," Earth thundered. "Humans will learn through fear what they can't learn through kindness."

Dismayed, Michael fell to his knees and pleaded, "I am but a servant to you, Great Spirit of Earth, but please, hear me. The children of men are just infants, impulsive and superstitious. Please give them more time. Please give them some guidance."

"We tried that," replied Earth. "Now be gone, both of you."

Michael returned to the place where the angels were buried. In the gray hours of dawn, Michael sat at Gabriel's grave under the olive tree and gasped with the pain of his grief.

*"That's a terrible story," said Fanny.*

*Michael nodded, "Earth punished me severely. I could not touch anybody without causing death, and nobody could see or hear me."*

*"But you did not do anything wrong," objected Fanny.*

*"But I would have; the snake was right. I would have partied all night and kissed every willing girl. The only reason I didn't do that was because nobody wanted me at the parties."*

*"What happened next?"*

*"Ten thousand years of solitude," Michael said.*

# Chapter Fifteen

# The Last of the Angels

For seven days, Michael sat on the ground next to Gabriel's grave. The people of Askalon walked past him, oblivious to his invisible presence. At first, Michael barely noticed the people; all he could think of were the bloodied and mutilated bodies of his brothers. But, as the days went on, he began to look at those who walked past him, but nobody returned his gaze.

"Hello," he said timidly, but the people paid him no attention.

"I am here," said Michael, but there was no response.

He returned to his perch under the tree and hung his head. At that moment, a white tomcat strolled by. It was a large animal with lush fur and brilliant green eyes. It looked at Michael and settled beside him, purring and rolling over to expose its soft belly.

"You can see me, big guy?" Michael asked, smiling at the animal, but when he gently touched the cat's head to pet it, it shrieked, convulsed, and was dead.

Michael stared at the lifeless lump of teeth and fur and gasped, "I am so sorry. I forgot that I kill every living thing I touch."

Michael got up and paced around his brothers' grave, mumbling to himself. "I cannot touch without killing, I cannot be seen, I cannot be heard, I am as a ghost."

He could not bear to stay in Askalon, where he had so many memories, so he abandoned the shack that had been his home and walked away. He traveled across valleys and hills, he wandered through fertile orchards and barren deserts, and he passed by rivers and lakes. He spread his wings and soared up to the clouds, hoping to rekindle the joy of flight he remembered, but the winds did not rock him, and the rains did not wet him, so he returned to the ground and continued on foot.

He walked through the fields, invisible to all women and men, without even casting a shadow. When he stepped on the grass, it withered under his feet. Flowers faded and lost their scent, and birds and insects fell silent when Michael approached.

Michael interrupted his wanderings only to follow the tug of his carrying bag and collect the souls of dying women, children, and men.

When Earth had first shown him the Space for Souls, it had been a simple room with a few alcoves and cushions, but as Michael brought in more souls, it expanded. In time, it had become a silent, endless maze of chambers and corridors, illuminated by a soft light that had no obvious source. Thousands of souls were sleeping in the safety of this space.

Michael floated weightlessly between the rooms and closed his eyes, trying to sleep. When sleep did not find him, he stopped by the pillow that held Jeema's soul.

"Hello, Jeema," Michael said, but the soul did not respond.

Michael sang a simple song to his childhood friend and gently caressed the soft, glowing sphere. The soul quivered a little under his touch but did not wake up.

One afternoon, as Michael brought in five new souls, he felt an insistent tug on his bag. It was much stronger than usual because it came from the souls of more than a hundred men, all killed at the same place and time.

The people of Askalon had again battled a neighboring tribe, and the bodies of the slain were strewn all over a field. The vegetation was burnt and soiled with the blood of war. Michael walked from corpse to corpse, gathering up the souls of the warriors, when he saw the Red Snake.

The snake glanced at Michael as it sank its fangs into a dead body. When the soul of the slain man appeared, the snake opened its jaws and devoured the soul. A tearing pain ripped through Michael's chest as he watched the soul disappear in the snake's maw.

"Stop it!" yelled Michael, but the snake only laughed and proceeded to the next corpse.

"You can't just destroy these souls," Michael sputtered, but the snake ignored him and went on to the next dead warrior.

"Those are the souls of good people, who were killed when they tried to defend their home," Michael pleaded, but the snake slithered on to its next meal.

Finally, the snake turned to Michael and said, "Earth gave me permission to catch flawed souls. These souls were all flawed. Yes, these men fell in battle, but they also beat their wives, they looted and stole."

Michael growled with anger and lunged at the snake.

"We are all done here, Angel of Death. Next time, be faster," said the snake as it disappeared in a cloud of rust-colored dust.

Michael shook his fists in the air, screaming in frustration and rage. Then, he took off, flying west.

Michael's body had grown - he now had the muscular body of a man and the sleek, powerful wings of a raven. He was a strong and skillful flyer, and he knew how to use the Space for Souls as a shortcut to any place in the world. It took him only a few hours to get to the Great Audience Hall.

The clearing was humming with the sounds of insects and birds. When Michael admired the blooms, they did not fade, and the air was heavy with the scent of flowers, moist dirt, and moss. Michael put his hands on some lichen hanging from an ancient tree, and it did not wither under his touch.

After an interminable time, he heard his mother's voice, "Michael, what brings you to my abode?"

Michael longed to see his mother's gentle brown eyes, but she was hiding her face, and there was only her voice.

"Mother," he pleaded. "The work you have assigned to me has become more than I can handle. The children of men are ever increasing in number."

"I will show you how to use the time of the world," responded Earth. "You may arrange all seven billion years of my life according to your needs."

A wind blew over Michael's face, and the secrets of time were laid bare in his mind.

"Are your concerns allayed now?" Earth asked.

Michael hesitated, then he pleaded, "I am lonely, Mother, and my solitude is more than I can bear."

"Oh, Michael," said Earth, and a small mist arose from the ground.

In the fog, Earth revealed herself in her form as the dark mother of Michael's childhood, with gentle brown eyes, long white hair, and a shawl of soft owl feathers.

As Michael fell to his knees, Earth smiled and opened her arms to her child. He leaned into her embrace, not wanting the moment to end.

"Mother, please don't be angry with me anymore," Michael whispered.

"I love you, my little Angel of Death, but you are made from the same faulty mold as the Angels of Light, easily corrupted and weak. I cannot allow you to touch human beings except to bring death. I will, however, let you touch other life."

"Mother, what if I touch someone by mistake?"

"If you make a mistake, know that your breath can restore life. But, Michael, use this power judiciously. Death is the fate that awaits every human, and a life stretched out over too much time brings sorrow and pain."

Then, the darkness descended upon Michael, and he was back in his shack in Askalon.

Years went by. Michael watched as humankind grew and advanced. The town of Askalon became a city, then the city was razed to the ground in a war, and another city sprang up nearby. Languages changed, kings and emperors came and went, and Michael collected his souls day after day.

"*You must have been so lonely,*" said Fanny.

"*Most of the time, I just focused on doing my job. One day at a time, as they say. But the solitude grew in my heart, and then, something happened that caused my world to come crashing down around me.*"

"*What happened?*"

# Chapter Sixteen

# Lost Souls

One day, when Michael went up to the Space for Souls, he noticed that some alcoves and cushions were empty. Michael, who knew every one of his souls by name, ran his hand across the bare alcoves and shook his head, uncomprehending.

He hastened to the next room and the next, counting the empty alcoves and cushions, when a cold fist gripped his heart.

"Jeema!"

He rushed to the room that had held Jeema's soul for so many years. Jeema's soul was not there.

Then, the image of the Red Snake slithered into his mind. The Space for Souls was supposed to be safe, a haven for souls where the snake couldn't get them, but Michael knew that the Red Snake was both hungry and wily.

The Space for Souls was not a physical place. It existed in the fifth dimension, spread over the whole of the galaxy, being everywhere and nowhere simultaneously. In order to leave the Soul Space, Michael had to think of a point on Earth where he wanted to be, and then he would appear ten thousand feet above that location.

Michael focused on the Great Audience Hall and emerged high above the ground, the endless jungle spread out below him. He threw himself into a daring dive. The wind rushed by his face, tossed his hair, and whistled through his wings. Michael alighted near the waterfall, ran up the slippery rocks that led to a hidden cave, flew through the darkness of the cavern, and emerged in the large clearing.

"Mother!"

The Audience Hall was peaceful, filled with the chirping of colorful birds and the humming of insects among the blooms. Small, white flowers grew in a billowing cloud around the polished tree stump, spreading their heady perfume. The silvery, old trees stood tall and silent, their translucent leaves swaying in a gentle breeze.

Michael, however, was not in the mood to admire the flora and fauna around him. He paced the clearing in circles, clenching and unclenching his fists.

"MOTHER!" he cried.

Earth appeared on the tree stump, sitting cross-legged, holding her staff across her legs. Her white hair fell to her hips, and she wore her green flowing robe and soft owl-feather shawl. She smiled at Michael and tilted her head.

"Michael," Earth said. "What's gotten into you?"

Too distraught to bow or to kneel, Michael blurted out, "Some souls are missing from the Space for Souls. I thought this was a safe place. Did the Red Snake get in there?"

"Oh, Michael," said Earth, gesturing for Michael to sit down next to her on the stump. "You do not remember? I explained it to you before, barely ten thousand years ago."

"Please explain it again," Michael stuttered, still standing. "And tell me that my souls are safe where they are."

"The souls are now waking up," Earth said. "And as they awaken, they make choices. Some choose to live their lives again to undo some mistakes. Some ask to be reborn in a new body. Some go straight to Nirvana. And a few, the most light-filled souls, are practicing for the Symphony of the Spheres."

"Ah." Michael sat down on the tree stump next to Earth. "So, they are safe?"

"No living thing is ever safe."

"And Jeema?"

"She chose a new body, obviously. She died at age nine and had no chance to live out her full life."

"How can I find her?"

"Go do your job, Michael. You have no business looking for Jeema."

*"Your mother is mean," said Fanny. "Why couldn't she let you have ONE friend?"*

*"She can be very stern," agreed Michael. "Sometimes I am deathly scared of her. But she has also been good to me. You don't choose your family, you know."*

*****

*"What is it like to fly?" Fanny asked the next night.*

*"There is nothing better than flying," Michael said. "Sometimes, I cross one of the oceans, just for the fun of it. I like it best when the waves are high, when there is thunder and lightning in the sky, and the winds are wild."*

*"Isn't that dangerous?"*

*"Not for me," said Michael. "I don't die unless my mother allows it."*

*"Fanny's eyes widened. "You could do ANYTHING."*

*Michael's eyes became unfocused. "That's not as great as you think. There were times I wanted nothing more than to die."*

*Fanny's eyes widened. "Did you try to off yourself?"*

*Michael shook his head. "That's not a story for a young child."*

*"Says who?" Fanny objected. "Grandma says that kids need to hear about the hard parts of life."*

*"Grandma said that?"*

*Michael took a deep breath.*

# Chapter Seventeen

# The Falling Angel

She could not have been more than ten years old. Her skin was olive, and her black hair was woven into a thick, single braid. She was alone, lying on her back, her emaciated frame covered with a thin, white sheet. Her dark cherry eyes stared at the ceiling. Michael gasped when he saw her; she looked so much like his Jeema.

He touched the girl's forehead and called her soul into his hands. He was almost relieved when he saw that it wasn't Jeema.

The translucent sphere quivered in the cold air. Michael gently stroked it, cooing to the trembling soul. He lowered the sphere into his carrying bag, where it would be protected from harsh sunlight and wind; then, he ascended.

At ten thousand feet, in the cold, thin air, his breath became labored, his vision faded, and his wings faltered. Then, there was a sense of falling, a jolt; the clouds around him vanished, and he was in the Space for Souls.

The maze of chambers, shelves, and alcoves was silent, and most of the cushions were empty. As Michael looked around the desolate halls, something inside him screamed.

He walked to the room where he had kept Jeema's soul for so many years. The red velvet of Jeema's abandoned cushion was threadbare and faded. He placed the new soul next to Jeema's old spot.

He looked down from ten thousand feet. Below him was a desert that stretched out as far as his eyes could see. The endless sand formed ripples and waves, glowing orange in the light of the evening sun,

"Ten thousand feet," Michael muttered. "Ten thousand years."

The years had passed slowly for Michael. He had gone about his duties in silence. Day after day, he had stepped to the deathbed of people who loathed him. He had collected souls from accidents, executions, murders, and plagues. He had appeared in earthquakes, fires, and floods. He had ripped souls from the bodies of children who were still warm in their parents' arms.

Like a wailing wind in the darkest hour of night, the pain and grief of his job had taken root inside him. The void in Michael's chest howled.

"Please, release me," he pleaded, but there was no answer.

There was no mercy for the Angel of Death.

The desolate land below him seemed lifeless, entirely given to death.

The noise in Michael's head thundered, "Die, Angel of Death, die. You deserve only to die."

He took off his belt and fastened it with the clip over his folded wings. Earth could always create another Angel of Death, the voice inside of him wailed.

Michael jumped.

As he fell, a primal fear took hold of him. His hands wandered to his belt, but it would not budge. The more he pulled at it, the deeper it dug into his wing feathers.

Michael closed his eyes. The wind whistled through his hair; the air was cold despite the sun's blinding glare. Then, the screaming inside his head faded. The howling void was no more. At the inevitable end of his existence, Michael felt a strange, serene moment of peace.

He hit the ground with a crushing thud. Pain seared through his neck and chest. He tried to breathe, but his lungs would not obey. Blackness descended upon him.

When he woke up, his neck throbbed, sending white-hot blades through his body. Michael sat up painfully, slowly, his sight obscured by red mist.

When the fog cleared, he saw his mother.

"Michael," Earth said. "What were you trying to do?"

"Mother," Michael rasped, fighting for air. "Please release me."

"I can never make another Angel of Death like you, Michael," Earth whispered to him.

"I am nothing," Michael said. "Please, let me go."

"You are the child of my heart, Michael. You are tenacious. You are compassionate. You will never abandon the souls in your care. None of the other angels could have done what you did all these years."

Earth blew her breath on Michael's broken neck, on the cracked ribs in his chest, and on his ruptured spleen. Then, she touched his temples, and the cold lump of despair inside his chest dissolved. Instead, there was an utterly unreasonable, inexplicable, small flame of hope.

Earth cradled her angel against her chest, and he fell asleep in his mother's warm arms.

He woke up in the Audience Hall. Eons had passed, or so it seemed to him. He was bedded on fragrant grasses and covered by Earth's owl-feather shawl.

Earth sat next to him on the ground, studying him silently.

"I may have been too harsh with you, Michael," she finally said. "Go find your Jeema. I will bestow a gift on her and all her offspring so that they will be able to see you."

Michael sat up and grasped his mother's hand. "You want me to find Jeema in her reincarnated form? But how will I know her?"

"She can see you, as I said. You will also sense a sweet pain in your heart. You will recognize it when it happens."

Michael leaned his head against his mother's shoulder and whispered, "Thank you, Mother."

On his way home, Michael took his time. He needed to think. He remembered his first trip across the ocean when he was just a child. The sea had been wild then, and Michael had barely made it across.

This time, though, the ocean was tranquil, and Michael sailed above small, white-crested waves carried by a gentle wind under his wings. He soared on thermals and coasted among the clouds. At times, the sun beat down on him; at other times, rain pelted him, but he did not mind. Jeema was alive, somewhere in the world, and Michael was going to find her.

He alighted in the City of Askalon and walked through its cobblestone streets. The city was mostly in ruins, but some people still lived here, selling trinkets to tourists. Memories of his childhood flooded his mind.

This could have been the street where Jeema had taught him how to play marbles. Here, she had given him his first bite of bread. His shack had been in a field like this, now overgrown with weeds.

Michael found a large house that overlooked the ocean. Gabriel had lived in a villa like this. Next to him had been Rafael's and Emmanuel's homes. Here was an olive tree like the one where Michael had buried his brothers.

And somewhere close by, in a house that no longer existed, Michael had collected Jeema's soul.

He sat on the old sandstone city wall. His longing, his need, and his solitude of ten thousand years surged in his chest and emerged as a scream.

"JEEEE-MAAA!" Michael wailed over and over again.

The sun hid behind thunder clouds, and the air became chilly. Lightning bolts appeared on the horizon, wind whistled through the alleys, and the first raindrops fell from the gloomy sky. The villagers could not see or hear Michael, but something in the air made them fearful.

"It's the Angel of Death, crying for his lost love," said the wise woman of the village.

The villagers shuddered; mothers grabbed their children and hastened into their homes. Soon, the streets were deserted.

When his voice was spent, Michael took to the sky and flew to the nearest big city. He walked through the marketplace, combed the playgrounds and schools, and searched the crowds at public events, walking, walking, hoping for that sudden light of recognition in the face of an olive-skinned girl. But the faces of the people in the streets were blank.

The years passed. Michael returned to his death-angel duties, collecting the souls of dying women and men. However, every day, after delivering his souls to the Beyond, he wandered the streets of towns and cities all over the world, searching for Jeema.

# PART THREE: FANNY'S FAMILY STORY

*"Did you ever find Jeema?" Fanny asked.*

*"Indeed, I did. She was a grown woman then, but still as sassy."*

*"Did you run into her in the marketplace?"*

*"No, it took twenty years of searching and hoping. Hope is such a strange thing. My mother could have simply led me to Jeema, but I guess she wanted me to earn this mercy."*

*"Did you recognize her right away?"*

*"It took me about five minutes."*

# Chapter Eighteen

## Jeema

One day, Michael found himself in a small rural hospital. He had been called to the deathbed of a young woman who had just given birth. Earlier in the day, the hospital room had been the scene of frantic activity, but now all the beeping machines had been removed, the doctors and nurses had left, and next to the blood-stained hospital bed, there was only a single infusion pole dripping saline into the patient's vein.

The young woman's life was seeping away in a relentless gush of half-clotted blood. The warm, red liquid pooled between her legs and filled the room with the stench of iron and rot. The bleeding had started with the first contractions and refused to stop even after the baby was born.

The woman was barely twenty. She had olive skin, now pale from the blood loss, and cherry-black eyes. Her smooth, dark hair spilled over her hospital gown.

The infant was premature, dusky, limp, too weak even to cry. The old doctor was sure that neither mother nor child would make it.

The midwife had put the listless newborn on her mother's bare chest and pulled the privacy curtains so that they could have a moment alone.

When the mother felt the warm, slippery body of her baby, she opened her eyes and gently caressed her daughter's wet hair. Then she looked up and saw the Angel of Death.

"Are you here for me?" the mother asked. "Please don't take my child."

She put both hands on her baby, trying to shield her daughter from the grasp of death.

Michael's eyes widened.

"You can see me!" the angel exclaimed. "Few mortals can."

"You did not answer my question," the mother grumbled.

"I am not here for the child," the angel said. "Not today."

At that moment. Michael felt a sweet pain in his heart. For a second, his breath stopped in his chest.

"Jeema?" Michael whispered, but the woman did not respond.

"What's your name?" Michael asked.

"Hannah," the woman said, struggling to sit up in her bed.

"A little help?" she asked. "Help me sit up, please."

"Afraid not," the angel said, taking a step back. "I can't touch you, or else."

The sweet pain in Michael's chest was almost too much to bear. No human eyes had seen him in ten thousand years. But for this dying young woman, he was real. It mattered if he smiled or frowned. His words carried weight. He did not want this moment to end.

Michael paused for a while, then he said, "I can make it so that your daughter will live. The Spirit of Earth gave me that power in case I touch someone by mistake. Unfortunately, there will be a price."

"Yes?"

"A soul whose life is stretched out beyond its decreed fate will suffer terrible sorrow and pain."

"Angel of Death, can you give me all the sorrow and pain that my daughter would have to endure, and let the child have a full life?"

The angel hesitated.

"Are you sure?"

"Quite sure. Do it already."

"This feels wrong," Michael muttered, but he bent over the baby and blew on her face.

The child shuddered and took a deep breath. A vigorous cry tore itself from the baby's throat, and the purple color of death left her body.

"I want to ask you a favor," the mother rasped.

The angel tilted his head and said nothing.

"I am sorry," Hannah continued. "I do not have anybody else I could ask. Please, will you watch over my child?"

"What about your husband?"

The woman shook her head and said, "He is not to be trusted."

The angel stood silent for a moment, then he nodded and said, "It would be my honor."

"What shall we call her?" Hannah asked.

The angel contemplated the baby for a while, and then he said, "I have always been partial to the name 'Diana.'"

"The Goddess of the Hunt?"

"Yes, that's the one."

"'Diana' it is," the woman said. "Dee-Dee for short, if you don't mind."

"Not at all."

"Is she your girlfriend?"

"Who?"

"Diana, the Goddess of the Hunt."

"She is just a myth," Michael said, then he blushed and added. "I have never had a girlfriend, but I have often wondered what it would be like to be kissed."

"Ah, yes, you can't touch, poor angel."

The woman paused for a moment, then said, "I'll kiss you if you want. I am ready."

The woman pursed her lips for a kiss, but the angel recoiled, frowning.

"Not so fast. I will have to extend your life, too, so you will have the years to bear your daughter's pain."

"The doctor said I would not make it," Hannah objected. "I am still bleeding. I'd be surprised if I had even a pint of blood left in me."

"Doctors!" the angel snorted. "What do they know? Most of them are too scared to face me."

He put his mouth within an inch of Hannah's face. Then he blew on her, and she gasped. She fought for breath for a good minute, snapping for air like a fish on land.

When her breathing finally calmed, she smiled at the angel and said, "Your breath smells bad."

"Consider what I do for a living," the angel protested.

"You may want to look into mouthwash," the woman said as she drifted off to sleep.

"Good night, Jeema," said Michael.

*"Wait," said Fanny. "The baby's name was Diana? Like my grandmother?"*

*Michael smiled. "Yes, this is your family's story."*

*"WOW," said Fanny. "I am the - wait - great-granddaughter of your Jeema, then?"*

*"Yes, you are."*

*"What happened next?"*

*"I stayed with Jeema through the few remaining years of her life. It was not easy to watch what I had done to her."*

# Chapter Nineteen

# Godfather Death

When Hannah returned home with her baby, she found her living room filled with flowers. The scent was overpowering. There were bouquets of red roses and sunflowers, hydrangeas in ceramic pots, and crystal vases full of fragrant jasmine.

Hanna's husband waited for her at the front door, his face grim. He was a stocky man with a protruding belly and barely any hair. He looked about twenty years older than Hannah.

"Who is sending you flowers?" he demanded to know before Hannah even had time to put Diana into her crib.

"I guess those aren't from you, then?" Hannah replied.

She looked around, and then she noticed Michael, who sat on a chair in the far corner of the living room, red-faced and smiling.

"You?" she hissed. "Are you trying to get me in trouble with my husband?"

"Who are you talking to, woman?" her husband growled.

Michael shrugged and lifted his hands in a gesture of helplessness.

"Nobody," said Hannah.

She picked up one of the cards affixed to a large bouquet of sunflowers and read, "For my Jeema. I missed you for ten thousand years."

"And why are all these cards addressed to 'Jeema?'" Hannah's husband thundered.

Hannah dropped the card and said, "There was a guy at the hospital. He saved my life, I think. He insisted that he knew me from another life, and my name had been 'Jeema' then. I swear there was nothing between us. The guy is crazy."

"Am not," said Michael.

A little later, when she was alone in her bedroom with her baby and Michael, Hannah took the angel to task.

"What were you thinking?"

"Jeema, I didn't mean to cause problems for you," Michael stuttered.

"I am not Jeema. I am Hannah."

Michael hung his head, "I am sorry. You have no idea what it means to be seen by someone, after all these centuries of being invisible. And then I find you, and you can see me. It's as if I am suddenly real. Forgive me."

Hannah studied Michael's face for a minute, then her expression softened. "You have been lonely."

Michael nodded.

"Aren't there any other angels who could keep you company?"

Michael shook his head, "No. They are all dead."

For a while, Hannah and Michael were silent.

"Fine," Hannah said finally. "You can call me 'Jeema' if that is your heart's desire. But no more flowers. No presents. You can't be courting me. And you can't be around unless I am alone. Is that understood?"

"I can be discreet."

"You can absolutely not be around me when there are other people. If people see me talking to you, they are going to think I'm crazy. My mother-in-law already hates me. Do you know what they do with crazy people around here?"

"Yes," Michael whispered. "OK. I'll stay away unless you are alone."

At that moment, the door to the bedroom opened. It was Hannah's husband who wanted to know who she was yelling at. Michael obligingly disappeared.

He was back the next day with a box of chocolates, which made Hannah growl like a tigress. "I said, 'No presents.'"

At that moment, the baby started to fuss.

"She needs a fresh diaper," Hannah said.

"Uhm," Michael said.

"You are useless!"

"I can't touch," Michael objected. "If I touch her bare bottom, I might kill her."

"You can always bring her back, right?"

"This kind of thing isn't done lightly," Michael said, his black feathers flustering.

"Figure it out," said Hannah.

"Fine," Michael grumbled and went to fetch diapers, baby oil, and wipes.

Then he carried Diana to the changing table using her bed sheet as a sling. He removed the baby's pants by gingerly pulling at the garment's toes. Next, he took off her dirty diaper, being careful not to touch her skin. So far, the operation proceeded without problems, but putting on a fresh diaper posed a new set of difficulties. Michael needed to lift the baby's butt to slide the diaper under her bottom. He finally solved the problem by tying a washcloth around Diana's ankles and pulling her feet up by the knot. Hannah stood three feet away and laughed hysterically at the sight of Michael trying not to kill his godchild.

"Couldn't you just wear gloves?" Hannah asked.

"Tried that," Michael replied. "The gloves become part of my person, and my touch, even with gloves on, still kills."

When night fell, Michael sat near Diana's crib and sang lullabies. Soon, the baby was fast asleep, and Hannah wanted to play cards.

"When you were nine, you taught me how to play marbles," Michael said, smiling at the memory. "Yes, let's play cards."

He paused, then he asked, "Can you teach me?"

Diana grew fast. She had her mother's smooth black hair and olive skin, but her eyes were as green as her father's. One night, when Diana was four, Michael heard a strange noise from the child's bedroom. The girl was awake, struggling to breathe, wheezing, unable to get one word out. She looked directly at Michael and mouthed the words, "Help." For a split second, Michael basked in the glow of Diana's gaze, then he rushed to Hannah's bedroom and yelled at her at the top of his lungs.

"Wake up, Jeema. Get Diana to the bathroom," he shouted. "It's the croup. She will die unless you make her breathe hot steam from the shower."

Michael had collected the souls of many young children with croup and knew what he was talking about.

Hannah jumped out of bed, startled. Her husband, who was snoring at her side, stirred but did not wake up. Hannah grabbed Diana, who was blue in the face and struggled to draw breath. Hannah turned on the shower, making the water as hot as possible, and rocked her daughter in her arms. After a minute, Diana's breathing became easier.

"Who is he?" Diana asked her mother a little later when she had her voice back.

"It's your guardian angel," said Hannah. "He is also the Angel of Death. His name is Michael."

"Mika-what?"

"Mee-kha-El. It means 'who is like God?' He told me that he was given this name to remind him that even the Angel of Death is but a servant. Few people can see him. I think it's because most people are too scared to take a good look."

"I am not afraid of him," said the child.

"Stay that way," said her mother. "I will not always be here."

*The next evening, Fanny eagerly awaited the next installment of her story.*

*"It's a pretty rough story. Are you sure you are ready to hear it?"*

*"Absolutely," said Fanny. "It can't be more gruesome than being swallowed alive by a wolf, now, can it?"*

*"Point taken," said the angel. "The next chapter is about Jeema's death."*

# Chapter Twenty

# No Torture Can Last Forever

A few years passed, and soon, much too soon, Hannah's life was ebbing away. Many days, she sat in her chair staring into space, unsmiling, unseeing. Michael stayed at her side, trying to cheer her up, but it was a rare day that he could get a word out of her. She no longer wanted to play cards. She barely ate, and all night, she lay in bed with her eyes wide open.

"Jeema, I am so sorry," Michael said. "I should never have restored your life. I was selfish. Forgive me if you can."

"How much longer, Michael?" Hannah whispered.

"Not that long, Jeema. If you want, I can take your soul right now."

"No, you can't. I am paying Diana's debt, am I not?"

"Yes, you are," Michael cried. "I should never have agreed to this bargain."

"Only a little longer," said Hannah. "For Diana."

One evening, twelve-year-old Diana found her mother with two bandaged wrists. When Diana asked what had happened, Hannah gave no response. That night, as Diana was doing her homework, the door to her room opened, and there was a choking sound. It came from her mother, who collapsed in front of Diana and breathed no more.

"NO!" yelled the girl when she saw the Angel of Death bend over her mother's still body.

The angel put his hands on her mother's forehead and gently, ever so gently, caressed her face. Between his hands, a sphere took shape. It scintillated in many colors and emitted a soft hum.

"Your mother had a beautiful soul," said the angel.

"Please don't take her," pleaded Diana. "Let her live. I love her. I need her."

"You would want her to continue like this?" asked the angel, and in the shimmering sphere, the girl saw her mother as she sat in her chair, staring at nothing, her wrists bandaged, her eyes black-rimmed and full of despair.

"She hung on as long as she could," said the angel. "She did that for your sake, dear child, but now she must be allowed to leave. No torture can last forever, and she has suffered enough."

At that moment, Diana's father burst into the room, alarmed by Diana's frightened scream.

"Call the ambulance," he yelled while he tried to breathe air into his wife's mouth.

He did not see the Angel of Death, nor did he hear his words. Diana ran to do as she was told, even though she knew it was futile.

That night, after her mother's body had been taken away, Diana sat in front of the house, staring into the night. The young man with the black wings sat next to her on the steps.

"I wonder where she is among the stars," Diana said.

"Everywhere," said the angel. "I know she is waiting for you in the Beyond."

The stars were silent; only the wind rustled in the bare branches of the nearby trees. The November air was cold with a hint of rain.

"Yes, she has nobody else," agreed Diana.

Fanny cried, "That is a REALLY sad story. Grandma must have been so sad."

"Yes, she was, but even the most terrible grief does not last forever."

Did you bring Jeema's soul to the Beyond?"

"Of course. I placed her in her old spot on a brand-new red velvet cushion. The weird thing is that a soul, once awakened, can stay awake. Jeema and I talk a lot. She asked me about the Symphony of the Spheres and about Nirvana. She still hasn't made up her mind, but she said she would wait for Diana before deciding what to do next."

"What happened to Grandma after her mother died?"

"Well, Diana's father was not one to do well on his own. At first, he tried to have Diana run his household, but eventually, that wasn't enough for him."

# Chapter Twenty-One

# The Stoneking's Wife

When Diana's mother died, Diana's father asked his daughter to keep their home tidy and clean. Diana scrubbed, cooked, and tended the garden. She was busy from morning to night, but she never complained because she adored her old father.

Then, one day, when Diana was barely eighteen, her father brought home a new wife.

He took Diana aside and said, "You have been a good, faithful daughter, but there isn't room in my house for two women. I have found a good man for you, so go, marry him, and be his dutiful wife."

Diana lived in a backward country where fathers arranged their daughters' marriages. The man her father had picked was much older than Diana, but he was rich, and the bride price he offered was high.

Diana did not like the man very much. It may have been the way he walked, with his back as stiff as a plank. Or it may have been that his eyes never smiled. But Diana had always obeyed her father, so she married the man.

Michael was not too sure about Diana's husband-to-be, so he found Diana in her bedroom as she was getting ready for bed.

"Diana, this man is no good," Michael said.

"Michael, this man will take me to a new land, away from the small minds and superstitions of this country. My daughters will grow up to be free."

"It is a mistake," Michael insisted.

"Michael, I know you mean well, but when I get to my new land, you must stay away. Please don't show yourself to me anymore. Don't talk to me. I want a new start, do you understand?"

Michael lowered his head and nodded, then he left Diana's room.

Diana and her new husband boarded a ship that took them across the ocean to a faraway place. The new bride brought only a bag with some clothes and a basket that held Little Toby, her dog.

When the woman saw her new home, she gasped in despair. The house was dilapidated, with peeling paint and a yard overgrown with brambles and weeds. The house smelled of garbage and mold. Heaps of clutter were piled up in every room. Even the kitchen floor was strewn with used paper towels, soiled underwear, dirty dishes, and a threadbare old coat.

"You told my father that you were rich," Diana exclaimed. "Yet you live in such filth?"

"I didn't get rich by spending my money on frivolous things," the man responded.

Diana asked her husband where she would sleep, and he showed her the bedroom. The bed was a mattress on the floor that reeked of years of hard use. On top of the mattress was a torn blanket and two sweat-soaked pillows. The young woman cried herself to sleep that first night with Little Toby, the dog, curled up in her arms.

The next morning, Diana began cleaning the house. It was an arduous task. Her husband's clutter was in the way, so she moved all his piles into one room, closed the door, and never set foot in that room again. She threw out the filthy mattress and bought a new one from a store in town.

The man was not pleased. He muttered through clenched teeth, slammed the door, and disappeared for a week. When he returned, he cast a disparaging glance at his wife's work but did not comment.

The man never had a good word for his wife, so she worked harder and harder, hoping to soften his heart. After a few months, the house smelled of cinnamon and roses, and the garden was lush with flowers and fruit. Alas, her husband's heart remained cold.

One night, as they lay in bed together, Diana caressed her husband's stubbly cheeks and nestled her head against his chest. Then she noticed a spot on his right arm. It was a hardened area the size of a hand, gray and cold to the touch. When she asked him about it, the man blanched.

"How are you able to see the patch?" he muttered between clenched teeth. "If you think that this gives you power over me, you will regret it; you will."

After that, the man refused to discuss his skin with her, and Diana watched with alarm as the stony patch grew day after day. Soon, it took over all of his arm. Slowly, the stone spread to his chest, but even then, the man would not see a doctor about it.

A year passed, and Diana gave birth to a baby girl. She named her Rowena, and the child was the joy of her heart; Diana rocked her in her arms, sang to her, and told her fantastic stories of fairies and elves.

When the weather was sunny, she took her child for walks in the woods, carrying the baby in a sling on her chest. One day, when she was exploring an ancient, dense forest, she stumbled upon a crystalline lake. She sat down at the shore and let her daughter play next to her on the sand. The girl's laughter rang out over the lake, and the birds sang overhead. For the first time since she had left her father's house, Diana felt peaceful.

A few months later, on a warm summer day, she and Rowena fell asleep at the lake, and when they woke up, it was late. At home, Diana's husband was waiting, enraged that his food was not on the table. In his anger, he hit Diana with his cold, stony arm. He beat her until her blood pooled on the kitchen floor.

The man's behavior worsened over time until, one evening, the man came home in a foul mood; he yelled and hurled dishes against the wall. Diana grabbed her five-year-old daughter, and they hid behind the sofa, trembling and silent as mice. The man looked around and, finding no one to hit, grabbed Little Toby, the dog. The dog yelped and struggled, but the man smashed its head against the wall and then dropped its lifeless form on the floor.

The next morning, when her husband had left for the day, Diana packed a bag with some clothes and toys, strapped Rowena into the car, and drove away.

She did not get far. Suddenly, her husband appeared on the road, tall as a tree and covered from head to toe in an armor of rock. He held out his hand against the car and stopped it with unnatural strength. The woman pushed on the gas, and the tires squealed, but the car would not move. The man's long, stony arm reached for the driver's side door, ripped it open, and yanked Diana out of her seat. He put his hardened hands around her throat.

Diana made peace with her God, but the man let go of her neck just as she was about to pass out.

As Diana lay on the ground, fighting for breath, little Rowena managed to unbuckle herself, jumped out of the car, and ran towards the man, yelling an eerie, howling wail. She kicked her father in the shin as hard as she could, rupturing the carapace. The fissure spread until the stone split open from bottom to top and fell off. In the ruins of the man's armor, there was a small, pale creature, slimy and covered with a thin, bloody smear. It barely resembled a man; its head was grotesquely large on its thin neck. It whimpered as it crawled in the dust, too weak to lift itself up.

Then, a giant red snake emerged from the bushes and slithered toward the weeping thing. It sank its fangs into the creature's chest, and its prey lay still.

At that moment, the Angel of Death made his appearance.

"Oh no," said Diana. "Michael, please don't."

"It's his time," said Michael. "I am sorry, Diana. I won't bother you again."

The angel knelt next to the small body and extracted the soul, but the sphere was crusted with pieces of rock, and there was no glow or hum. In the angel's hands, the sphere disintegrated and rained to the ground as a shower of sand.

The Red Snake, which had been waiting expectantly at the side of the road, approached and licked up every kernel of sand, and then it slithered away.

"Who were you talking to?" Rowena asked her mother.

"It's the Angel of Death," said Diana.

"There is nobody there," said Rowena. "Let's go."

Diana staggered to her feet, got behind the wheel, and took off.

*Fanny's eyes were wide as she listened to the tale, "So, my mother, Rowena, killed her own father?"*

*"Not really," said the Angel of Death. "It was his time. His carapace of stone was about to disintegrate even without the kick. Unfortunately, Rowena never understood that, and the guilt made her take a bad path."*

# Chapter Twenty-Two

# The Stoneking's Daughter

Diana and her daughter traveled for many days until they reached the far end of the land. There, for a while, Diana lived peacefully with Rowenna. But one day, she noticed a tiny gray spot on her daughter's elbow. Diana clung to the hope that the spot on Rowena's arm would not grow, but it did.

The child began to lie and steal. She terrorized the neighbor's kids, chasing the smaller ones with a baseball bat. One day, she snuck into the neighbor's yard and tried to stomp on their young puppy. Diana and Rowena had to move because the neighbors threatened to take Diana to court.

Diana brought her daughter to doctors, but nobody else was able to see the gray patch.

One doctor said, "She is starved for attention."

Another doctor told Diana that her daughter needed more praise. A third recommended more freedom. Diana earnestly followed all this advice, but the girl did not improve.

One day, when Rowena was eighteen, she got drunk and brought three young men into the house. She hid them in the basement closet. When her mother found the boys in the morning and saw their vomit all over the floor, she sent the boys home and yelled at her daughter.

By then, the patch on Rowenna's elbow had encased her whole arm.

Diana broke out in tears and whispered, "You are of the stone."

Rowena flew into a rage.

"I am not of the stone," she snarled. "You are the one who is made of stone."

The girl lunged toward her mother and reached for her throat. Diana stood very still.

"I know how to disarm you," Diana said. "One hard kick to the shin will do. Leave now and never come back."

When Diana was alone at last, she got into her car and drove. She drove with no thought of where she was going. Then, after many weeks on the road, she realized that she was near the ancient forest. She found the crystalline lake, and there, she put up her tent. In time, she built herself a hut and planted a garden. She fished and swam in the lake. In the shade of the trees, she listened to whispering sounds in the canopy.

Then, one day, as she sat by the water and watched the sun dip into the lake, she heard a soft, whining sound nearby. It came from a tiny black pup who had crawled out from under the bushes. It was hungry and wanted some of her fish. The little dog jumped on her lap.

"And who might you be?" asked Diana.

When the dog did not answer, she said, "I'll call you 'Little Toby the Second,' if you don't mind, and I will take very good care of you."

The little dog licked her face and fell asleep, curled up in her lap.

*"Poor Grandma!" exclaimed Fanny. "Did you bring her the puppy?"*

*The angel blushed and nodded. "Diana needed someone to love."*

*"That was good of you. But I have so many questions. Where did the patch of stone come from? And what about that snake? There is a lot missing in that story."*

*"Yes, the Stone King Origin Story," sighed the Angel of Death. "It's the story of your grandpa when he was a boy."*

# Chapter Twenty-Three

# The Stoneking's Origin

There was a boy who was terrified of many things. He was scared of snakes, dogs, rats, dragons, lions, and his older sister, but the things he feared more than anything else were school buses. School buses looked like yellow monsters to him, with glowing headlights for eyes and ravenous, tooth-filled grille coverings for mouths. He hated the way their engines roared and the poisonous stench of their diesel fumes. His mother had to walk him to school every morning because he refused to go by himself.

The boy's mother was a poor widow who was angry about her lot in life. She told her children that their father was rotting in hell. One day, as his mother was going on and on about the evils of men, the boy noted that darkness was falling inside the house even though the time of day was noon. The walls seemed to creep in on him, and the air was thick with dust and debris. The boy tried to run, but the door was stuck. He rattled the door handle, which suddenly seemed to be made of stone. The door itself had become as heavy as a marble slate. The boy screamed and pushed with all his might. When finally, the door budged, he ran into the sunshine outside, whimpering with fear.

Sometime later, his mother fell ill and said, "Son, I am too sick to bring you to school today. You can either stay home with me or go on your own."

The school was only three blocks away, and the boy did not want to stay home with his mother and listen to more stories about the evils of men, so he decided to walk by himself. He took a deep breath and stepped onto the sidewalk in front of the house. When nothing bad happened, he took a few more hesitant steps, and then he ran.

He had covered half the distance to school when he saw a huge snake on the ground. Its flaming red scales were glistening in the sun. It had long, brownish fangs and a forked tongue that flicked in and out of his mouth.

The snake looked at the boy with its slitted, yellow eyes and hissed, "Hello, little boy. Why are you all alone today?"

"Go away," the boy said and ran to take cover behind a garbage can.

"There, there," the snake said. "I am not going to hurt you, at least not yet. I have a deal for you."

"A deal?" the boy asked, peeking out from behind the garbage can. "How do you even speak?"

"Here is the deal," the snake hissed. "I know that you are scared of everything."

The snake puffed itself up and suddenly looked like a giant rat with a filthy coat. It had an overpowering stench of decay. The rat whipped its naked tail at the boy; then it turned into a mangy dog the size of a cow. The dog's ugly mouth was drooling a liquid half spit and half blood. The dog's eyes were hungry; it snarled and crouched for a jump. The dog did not get to jump, though, because suddenly it became a school bus, sickly yellow and flashing its headlights. The bus stank of diesel and revved its engine at the boy. The boy shrieked in fear.

Then, the school bus became a snake again and continued in a soothing voice, "I can give you armor that will make all your fears go away. Want to try? The first time is free. Just speak the words, 'Stone King.'"

"Stone King," said the terrified boy, who would have grasped at any straw.

Suddenly, all his terror was gone, and the snake shrank to the size of a little earthworm. He picked it up in his hand and tickled its belly. The snake jumped down from the boy's hand and grew back to its original size.

"Does this armor make me invincible?" asked the boy.

"Not really. It makes you fearless, and that gives you power. But the armor has a weak spot. A swift kick against your shin will destroy it and kill you."

"You said the first time is free," the boy said. "So, what's the price for the second and third times?"

"Two things," said the snake. "Every time you invoke the Stone King, a patch of gray stone will grow on your skin. But don't worry, only those of the Stone can see it."

The snake paused, then added, "Those who love you can sometimes see it, too."

"And the second part of the price?"

"Your soul, of course," the snake said. "Nothing is free in this world."

"Go away," the boy said. "You cannot have my soul."

"I can't have your soul?" laughed the snake. "Well, maybe, maybe not. The stone grows every time you call on the Stone King. But I can get to your soul only if you allow the stone to spread to your heart."

"So, if I use my armor only a few times, you can't have my soul?"

"That's correct," the snake said, then slithered away.

The boy walked the rest of the way to school and noticed he wasn't scared at all. Even his stern old teacher looked shriveled and weak. When the boy was called to read his homework aloud, he did not hesitate for a moment. The other kids applauded when he was done, and the teacher gave him a warm smile.

"I knew you had it in you," she said.

But by the time classes ended, his armor had faded. There were school buses everywhere; they all seemed to follow him with their glowing eyes. Any moment now, one of them would rev its engine and try to run him over. The boy ran home as fast as he could.

When he arrived at his house, sweaty and all out of breath, he bumped into his older sister. She called him a nitwit, pulled him by the hair, and tried to stuff his head into the toilet.

"Stone King," yelled the boy.

Suddenly, he felt bigger and stronger, and his sister looked like a garden gnome.

He hit her squarely in her face and said, "Leave me alone, you bully."

His sister ran away crying, and the boy stepped in front of the bathroom mirror to examine his body from head to toe. Just as the snake had said it would happen, there was a little gray spot near his right elbow. It was the size of a small coin, hard as stone, and cool to the touch.

From that day on, the boy measured the patch every day, reassuring himself that it was far from his heart. He did not notice that the stone grew on his soul all the while.

"So, both Grandpa and Mom made a pact with the Red Snake?" Fanny asked.

The Angel of Death nodded, "Rowena did not have an easy life, and not a long one either, but it ended well for her."

"She died young - how can that be a good end?"

"Her soul did not turn into sand, like her father's soul did. Rowena's soul wasn't perfect, but souls don't need to be perfect. A flawed soul can decide to live her life again and correct some mistakes."

"Do I have a flawed soul?"

"You have a young soul, and as far as I can tell, it's damn near perfect. The challenge is to keep it that way when you grow up."

# Chapter Twenty-Four

# Rowena's Baby

The young woman staggered across the grassy field, holding her dead baby in her arms. She was dressed in a blood-stained hospital gown and barefoot. Her curly black hair was uncombed and fell in her face. She was shivering in the cool autumn morning.

"Mi-cha-el!" she yelled. "Mi-cha-el. Goddamn you, show yourself."

As the young woman struggled on the uneven ground, the air in front of her coalesced into the shape of a young man — if you would call him a man. He had a large pair of raven-black wings, and his hair and clothes were equally black. The angel scrutinized the young woman for a moment.

"Rowena," said the Angel of Death. "You called my name? Do you know who I am?"

"You are the Angel of Death," responded the young woman. "My mother once told me your name."

Rowena stared at the angel, her face distorted with rage.

"Bring her back," she demanded.

"Bring back your baby?" the angel asked.

"Yes, of course. Bring her back to me. You had no right to take this innocent soul."

"I can't, I am sorry," said the angel.

He reached under his right wing and produced a bag made from a delicate, iridescent fabric.

He peered into the bag and retrieved a sphere from it, put it back, fished out another one, and put it back, too, all the while mumbling and shaking his head, "Not this one, not this one either, ah, yeah, here she is."

The sphere he held in his hands was smaller than the other spheres he had examined. It had a soft, even glow, and it hummed a very simple tune.

"This is your baby's soul," said the angel. "Have a closer look."

The young woman peered at the sphere, and in it, she saw scenes of a life. The girl in one scene was in a hospital bed, screaming in pain, and then she was in a wheelchair, her grotesquely contorted limbs twitching uncontrollably. The child's mother entered the room, and the girl yelled that she hated her mother. While Rowena watched, the glow of the soul became dimmer and dimmer, until all the light within it went out.

"This is the life she would have had had she not died," said the angel.

Rowena looked stricken.

"She is all I have," she said.

"How are you even able to see me?" asked the angel. "I know you have the gift, but you have always been too scared to look me in the eye."

"I invoked the Stone King," admitted the young woman. "It takes away my fear. I made a pact with a very large snake that I would lose my fears for a short while if I invoked the Stone King."

"And the price?"

The young woman held out her right arm to show that it was encased in a carapace of stone.

"When the stone reaches my heart, I will die. I know that, yet I don't seem to be able to stop myself. I invoke the Stone King almost every day."

The Angel of Death ran his hand up and down near the young woman's chest, being careful not to touch.

"It's not your heart you should worry about. It's your soul that is turning to stone."

"I know," said the young woman. "I can feel it. That's why I wanted a baby so much. I need someone to love, someone who will save me from the stone."

"I have a proposal for you," the angel said, smiling at the young woman. "I can cure you of the stone, but in return, you will have to serve as my apprentice for a while. You will be invisible to most people, and you will help me collect souls."

"And when my apprenticeship is over?"

"You will return to being an ordinary human, to live out your short life free of the stone."

Rowena sat down on the wet grass, still cradling her dead baby in her arms.

Then she put her child's body on the ground and said, "I am ready if you would help me bury her, please."

Suddenly, the young woman felt as light as a feather, and she had charcoal-colored wings on her shoulders. Her hospital gown disappeared, replaced by a black robe with a wide opening on the back to accommodate the wings.

"Shoes?" asked the young woman.

"Of course," grumbled the angel, and Rowena's feet were now in sensible, flat-heeled black shoes.

The Angel of Death picked up the dead baby, and in his arms, the body disappeared.

"I put her in the same graveyard where your father was buried," the angel said. "Now come, see what I do for a living."

The angel and his apprentice materialized in a hospital room where an old woman was wheezing and choking in her bed. There was nobody with her.

"She is dying," explained the Angel of Death.

"Of course," said Rowena, "Otherwise, you wouldn't be here, right?"

The angel nodded, "She has a very bad temper. All the nurses are scared of her. Yesterday, she threw her breakfast at a nurse."

"Why is she so angry?" Rowena wanted to know.

"That's an excellent question that nobody has bothered to ask. Why don't you find out?"

The young woman felt how gravity took hold of her body again, and her pair of black wings disappeared. She sat down next to the dying woman's bed and smiled shyly.

"Hello."

"Who are you?" growled the old woman. "Go away."

"Why are you so grumpy?' Rowena asked.

"You'd be grumpy, too, in my place. I went to the hospital because I had a little cough, and they told me that my whole body was riddled with cancer. They don't even know where the cancer originated. They gave me four weeks, and now they tell me that they want to send me home like that."

"Would you rather stay in the hospital?'

"Of course. I have nobody at home, and my only son hasn't talked to me in years."

Rowena took the old woman's hand in hers, hoping that her touch wouldn't kill her, but apparently, her death-angel powers were suspended for now.

"What scares you most about dying?" the young woman asked.

"Dying alone," muttered the old woman.

"That's not going to happen," said the angel's apprentice. "I'll see if we can find your son, and if not, I'll stay with you as long as you need me."

"Four weeks!" exclaimed the dying woman. "Four weeks; I don't believe this. I felt just fine a week ago."

"You may yet surprise us all," said the apprentice. "Doctors don't know everything."

The old woman smiled a little, and then she fell asleep. Rowena went looking for the head nurse.

"I can't believe she let you talk," said the nurse who took Rowena to be one of the ever-changing interns. "She has been nothing but mean to us. Everybody avoids her room."

Rowena smiled. "Do me a favor and find her son."

"I'll sic our social worker on it," the nurse promised. "Can you keep visiting her? Please?"

"Of course," said Rowena

From then on, the young woman visited the dying patient every day. She sat with her, holding her hand, and asked about the woman's best memories. Then, one day, as she was feeding her patient a little broth, the door opened, and in walked a bearded young man.

"Mother!"

Rowena smiled at the son and tiptoed out of the room. When she closed the door softly, she saw mother and son hugging and sobbing.

After four weeks, the old woman died with her son at her bedside, holding her hand.

"This wasn't so bad," said Rowena when Michael picked her up from the hospital lobby. "Do you have more cases?"

"More than I care to count," said the angel. "Let's go and see the man who is about to kill himself."

The angel led his apprentice to the psychiatric ward and pointed out a young man who sat alone in a corner, brooding and muttering to himself. Rowena noted that she had retained her wings and was invisible to the people on the ward.

"You want me to persuade him not to jump?" asked the apprentice.

"Just talk to him," said the angel. "Don't worry. He is the only one here who can see you."

"Nobody cares," said the patient. "They'll let me out tomorrow, and I will jump from the highest building in this godforsaken city."

"Why?"

"Why? Because I am tired. I can't work; my body is ruined by too many drugs. My mother cries her eyes out about me every day. It's time she gets some peace."

"What do you think happens to you after you die?" asked the young woman.

"There will be silence and darkness. That's all I want – silence and darkness."

Rowena tried every way she could think of to talk him into choosing life, but the man did not budge.

"You are just a figment of my imagination, my pretty little Angel of Death. I am not afraid of dying."

"What is it then that scares you?" asked the apprentice.

The young man did not answer but said, "Will you stay with me when I take that last step and when I fall, fall so deep? Be with me, will you?"

"I will," said the young woman, wiping tears from her eyes. "Nobody should die alone."

The next day, the young man stood on the roof of the tall parking garage and looked down at the pavement below.

"I need to make sure I don't hit someone when I land," he said. "Please, pretty Angel of Death, give me a count of three when the moment is right."

"I can't do that," Rowena cried out. "It would be like killing you myself!"

"Nonsense," said the young man. "You'll save someone down below, that's all."

"Three – two – are you sure?"

"Yes, Angel of Death, I am sure."

"One," said Rowena, and the man jumped.

He fell with Rowena flying next to him, unseen by all but the falling man. His eyes were fixed on Rowena's face.

"You are gorgeous," the man said to Rowena, then he hit the ground.

"I don't know if I am cut out for this job," sobbed Rowena when Michael joined her on the pavement to retrieve the man's soul.

"You did well," said the angel. "Tomorrow, I will take you to the scene of an earthquake."

Seven years passed, and the Angel of Death brought his apprentice to the same grassy field where they had met a long time ago. As the young woman stood in the afternoon sun, her black wings dissolved into the air. Rowena looked much healthier now. Her glossy black curls were held back in a ponytail. Her face was a little chubby with pink, heart-shaped lips and chocolate-brown, expressive eyes.

"Your years of service in my employ have come to an end. You are free to go," said the angel.

"Where will I go?" the young woman asked. "I killed my father, and I hurt my mother so badly that I might as well have killed her, too. There is no forgiveness for someone like me."

"Have you asked for forgiveness?" the angel said, his voice gentle and soft.

"I don't even know where my mother lives," the young woman objected.

"Are you scared?" asked the angel.

"Yes," said the young woman.

"That's good. Note how your body is now free of the stone. Fear feeds the Stone King, but what you need is not the absence of fear. The secret is to be afraid and do what's good and right anyway."

"Can you help me find my mother?" the young woman asked. "I don't think I have enough years left to find her without your help."

"That I can do," agreed the angel. "But after that, we need to part ways, much as I have enjoyed your company."

When the sun rose the following day, Rowena stood by her mother's hut at the crystalline lake. She remembered this lake. Her mother had taken her to play there when Rowena was little.

The young woman knocked at the door and softly called out, "Mother!"

Diana, now an old woman, answered the door. She was wearing a coarse gray robe and had her long white hair woven in a single braid. A small black dog kept close to the old woman's left leg.

Diana gasped, "Rowena! Didn't I ask you to leave and never come back?"

The young woman fell on her knees and whispered, "Forgive me."

Diana helped her daughter get up and scrutinized her face. She ran her hand over the young woman's right arm and, finding no hardened spots, smiled.

"I already forgave you, my child," the old woman said. "Come inside. I have some excellent peppermint tea from my garden."

The young woman stayed with her mother for a while, but one day, Diana took her aside and said, "I love your company, Sweetheart, but this is no life for a young woman. You must go and find a job, meet a good man, and maybe have a family of your own. I will be okay, as long as you visit me from time to time."

So, Rowena left her mother's hut and walked all the way to the big city. After hiking for a day and a half, she spotted an enormous red snake at the side of the road. Rowena's heart wanted to stop, but she forced herself to put one foot in front of the other.

"I see you have abandoned our agreement," the snake hissed. "You will pay for that betrayal, as I am sure you know."

"There is no betrayal," the young woman said firmly. "The contract was that I could invoke the Stone King to get over my fears. It did not say that I HAD to invoke him. You are a liar. I will stay free of you."

"The armor would prolong your life," the snake said. "Do you not fear death?"

"Not much," said the young woman and laughed. "The fear of death is the source of all fears. Go away. You cannot have my soul."

Two years later, Rowena returned to her mother's hut at the lake. In her arms, she carried her six-month-old baby. The baby was a strapping girl who babbled happily and grabbed at her mother's black curls with strong little hands.

The young woman placed the girl in her mother's arms and said, "Mother, this is my daughter, Fanny. Please take good care of her because my time on Earth is up. The Angel of Death is waiting for me outside the hut."

Diana cradled the baby in her arms and shook her head. "You are young, Rowena. How can your time be up?"

"Leukemia," Rowena said. "I have known for a while. Michael wiggled the strands of fate to give me time to bring Fanny to you, but even he cannot stretch the threads any farther than this."

Diana sighed. "He did the same thing for my mother. One day, he will get himself into trouble, I fear."

Diana opened the door and shouted, "Come on in, Michael."

When the angel stepped through the door, Rowena smiled, "Michael, I served you loyally for seven years. Now, can I ask you a favor?"

The angel tilted his head, saying nothing.

"Will you look out for my baby?"

"It would be my honor," the Angel of Death said. "Are you ready, Rowena?"

When the young woman nodded, he caressed her face and caught her as she collapsed on the floor. A translucent sphere appeared in the angel's hands. The sphere was mottled in places and glowing in others. It showed no trace of the stone.

*Fanny was crying. "Is Rowena waiting for Diana in the Beyond?"*

*"Mothers and daughters tend to wait for each other in the Beyond. Sometimes, I have to expand the waiting rooms to accommodate five generations."*

*"The baby was me?"*

*"Yes. You were entrusted to your grandmother and me."*

*Michael's eyes softened as he thought back to that moment when Rowena collapsed in his arms, beautiful, raven-haired Rowena, his marvelous apprentice. He had let her go after seven years, as he had promised, but he would not have minded having her with him for all the years of his life.*

*Fanny smiled through her tears, "Good night, Godfather Michael."*

# Chapter Twenty-Five

# Little Boats Adrift

Eight-year-old Fanny came home sobbing. Her eyes were red, her lids were swollen, and her nose was dripping copious amounts of snot. Michael, who had picked her up from school, could not get her to utter a single coherent sentence. She cried and carried on, and when she finally stopped bawling, she refused to look at Michael and did not say a word. And as soon as they entered Grandma's house, the crying started all over again.

Grandma, of course, came running.

"She is crying and crying," Michael said. "And she won't tell me what it's all about."

Grandma made hot apple cider for Fanny and took her on her lap, but even in Grandma's arms, it took half an hour before the truth came out. There was a birthday party for one of the girls in school, and Fanny had not been invited.

Grandma wiped Fanny's nose with her apron and asked, "Do you even like that kid?"

"No," Fanny sobbed. "She is stuck up and mean."

"So, why do you want to go to the party then?"

"That's not it. I was not invited because the other kids don't like me. They say I am weird."

"How so?" Michael asked.

"It's your fault," Fanny hissed, glaring at Michael. "They have heard me talk to you when you walk me to school, only they can't see you, so they think I am crazy."

Michael blushed, "I am sorry. Maybe I should not walk you to school anymore?"

"Or at least don't talk!" Fanny snapped.

Michael hung his head, nodded, and left the room.

"Fanny," Grandma said. "I think you need to apologize to your Godfather. He is trying to be there for you."

"I want a real Dad."

"Your Dad died before you were born, Fanny. He was a good man, but he is gone."

"Michael is just a ghost. Nobody can see him, and he has never, ever, not once, given me a hug."

"He can't," Grandma sighed. "Every person he touches dies. He is the Angel of Death, after all."

"Some father figure," Fanny snorted.

The next day, Fanny insisted on walking to school by herself. The elementary school was not that far – one mile down the road. On the way, Fanny kicked some pebbles and ripped out some of the tall, flowering grasses. The vegetation was moist from the morning rain. Fanny shivered in the cool autumn air. When she reached the village, she passed by old Mr. Miller's house.

Mr. Miller, a gray-haired, gnarly man, was on his knees, pulling weeds. He wore dungarees and a checkered red shirt. His sparse gray hair was matted with sweat. When he saw Fanny, he smiled and tried to get up from his kneeling position. Getting up was quite the production, though. Mr. Miller put one foot in front of himself, leaned forward, clung to a nearby fence post, and heaved his body into an upright position. Fanny thought she heard Mr. Miller's joints groan and creak.

"Hi there, little Miss Fanny," he wheezed. "Would you like some hot chocolate?"

Fanny knew Mr. Miller well and loved his treats, so she nodded, "Yes."

The old man limped into his house and returned with two steaming mugs. Fanny and Mr. Miller sat side by side on the porch swing and sipped hot chocolate with little pieces of marshmallows on top.

"So, where is your imaginary friend today?" Mr. Miller asked.

Fanny almost dropped her cup and stuttered, "Imaginary friend?"

"Oh, come on, I hear you talk to him all the time."

Mr. Miller grinned, then added, "I had an imaginary friend, too, when I was little."

"Really? What was his name?"

"Legolas, like the elf. I was a Lord-of-the-Rings fan."

"Did you ever get teased about him?"

"Plenty, but Legolas was my friend. He helped me a lot. You do not give up on a friend just because of a little teasing."

"Mine is called Michael. And he isn't human either."

"Really! What is he?"

"He is an angel. The last of the angels, actually."

Mr. Miller's eyes widened, "You've got quite the imagination."

"He is my Godfather. And he is the Angel of Death."

"I wish I could see him." Mr. Miller thought for a moment. "I think only a few very special people can see the Angel of Death. If I were you, I would hide him from the other kids, but never, ever send him away."

"How did Legolas help you if he was just imaginary?"

"He was the voice of something buried inside me, a wisdom I did not know I had. Nowadays, they call it the subconscious. He saved me from a lot of stupid decisions."

"When did he leave you?"

"Who says he ever did?" Mr. Miller smiled. "It is true that there were years when I did not talk to Legolas at all, but one day, when I was in a rough spot, I begged him to come back."

"A rough spot?"

"My marriage was going downhill, and I was scared of being left all alone."

"So, Legolas came back?"

"Yes, and he told me not to be afraid of being alone. He said that aloneness is an existential condition and not to be feared."

"A what?"

"Every human being is alone, but most don't know it. We are like little boats, adrift on a vast, black ocean at night. Sometimes, we float alongside another boat, and we may talk to each other for a while. But we are still tiny boats lost on this large, large body of water. When we sink, we sink alone. And it is all good."

"How can this be good?!" Fanny exclaimed.

"Ask your angel about it. The Angel of Death is the loneliest of all creatures. He understands."

That evening, when Fanny returned home, she walked up to Michael and said, "I am sorry, Michael. I was scared that I would never have any friends. Please don't leave me."

"You spoke to Mr. Miller, didn't you?" Michael said with a little smile. "He is almost ready to meet me."

Michael paused, glancing at Grandma, who smiled and nodded at him.

"Would you like to come with me to collect his soul when it is time?" he asked.

Fanny's eyes widened. "Yes, I want to see how you collect souls."

She paused, "But does it have to be Mr. Miller? I love this old man."

"Everything ends, Fanny," Michael said softly.

The next day, Michael walked Fanny to school. They stopped at Mr. Miller's house, but the old man was not in his yard. They found him asleep on his couch. When Fanny approached the sofa, the old man opened his eyes and smiled at Fanny. Then he gasped.

He was looking directly at Michael and said, "Are you the Angel of Death?"

"Indeed, I am," Michael replied. "How is it that you can see me?"

"I always wanted to see you," said Mr. Miller. "You are beautiful."

Fanny ran to Mr. Miller and gave him a hug. "Please don't go yet. I love you so much."

"Don't be afraid, Fanny. It is my time. Everything is as it should be."

Michael knelt next to the couch and gently touched the old man's forehead. Mr. Miller sighed, closed his eyes, and became very still.

His soul appeared as a translucent sphere in Michael's hands. It emitted a warm light and had patterns in many colors swimming across its surface.

"Can I touch it?" Fanny asked.

Michael nodded, and Fanny gently stroked the warm globe. Then she heard a faint hum.

"This is the music of his soul," Michael said.

Fanny looked at the lifeless body on the couch, and suddenly, for a fleeting moment, she knew that there was no need for fear, none at all.

# PART FOUR: FANNY GROWS UP

*The years passed. Fanny was sixteen and had outgrown Michael's bedtime stories. Michael no longer walked her to school, and Fanny banished Michael from the living room every time she had friends over so that she would not be tempted to talk to him. Michael shrugged tolerantly and complied. When the sun was out, he and Diana hung out in the yard with coffee and apple cake. When the weather was bad, they played cards in Diana's bedroom.*

*One evening, after all of Fanny's friends had left, Michael took Fanny aside and asked, "Have you thought about what you want to be when you grow up?"*

*Fanny shrugged, "I like writing."*

*"You can do that, too," the angel said. "But I think you would make a good doctor."*

*"Pfff," Fanny said.*

*"I have a story about a girl who wanted to be something else," Michael said.*

*Fanny put her feet on the coffee table and grinned, "Go ahead, Godfather Death."*

# Chapter Twenty-Six

# Linnea and the Seven Firefighters

Linnea's day started badly. There was a power outage, so the alarm clock didn't go off, and Linnea got dressed in a rush and in the dark. She was wearing mismatched socks, crumpled-up pants, and a stained, yellow T-shirt. She had her greasy brown hair in a ponytail so that it wouldn't fall on her face.

Between driving her daughter, Cindy, to school, running half a dozen errands, picking up Cindy from school, dropping her off at kickboxing classes, taking Fido to obedience school so that he would stop peeing on the carpets, racing back home to make dinner, Linnea had no time to shower or change into cleaner clothes. The day got even worse when Linnea realized that she needed onions for dinner, only to find that the convenience store down the road did not carry onions.

Now, she was stirring the pot of stew without onions when Cindy walked in and declared, "I am going to be a firefighter."

"Sure," said Linnea, "Can you let Fido out, please?"

Cindy was a bouncy nine-year-old with flaming red curls who loved to wrestle with other kids.

"I mean it," said Cindy. "Can you enroll me in firefighter school?"

"You need to be a little older for that," said Linnea, brushing a stray strand of hair from her eyes.

Cindy sat on the floor and frowned, pushing her lips out in a well-practiced pout.

"I talked to Dad about it. He said it's a man's job. Why can't girls be firefighters?"

"Well, it's a very dangerous job," said Linnea.

"So?"

"And you need to be strong."

"I am."

"Well, if Dad says you can't be a firefighter, then that's it," said Linnea, hoping that would end the conversation.

She had no such luck; the meltdown came right on cue. Cindy ran to her room, slamming the door and screaming that she hated her mother and wasn't going to eat dinner. Then she yelled that if she starved to death, it would be her mother's fault.

At that moment, Linnea's mother-in-law, Ursula, descended the staircase and threw Linnea a glance of utter contempt. Ursula was perfectly coiffed, wearing an elegant white pantsuit. Linnea noticed that her mother-in-law's makeup was impeccable, with just the right amount of mascara and rouge.

"You have one child," Ursula said. "One, and you can't make her happy? What kind of a mother are you?"

Ursula was currently visiting, although "visiting" was not the right word to describe it. Ursula had moved in three months ago and showed no sign of wanting to leave.

Linnea took a deep breath and tried to focus on dinner. Ursula bent over the pot, sniffing and contorting her face in disgust.

Linnea balled her fists but said nothing.

The next morning, when Linnea was frying bacon and boiling eggs, Cindy planted herself in front of her mother and said, "I am going to be a firefighter."

Linnea was about to say something noncommittal when Cindy blurted out, "Just because you have no career doesn't mean I can't have one."

"Now, wait a minute," said Linnea. "I work very hard. I take care of the house, you, the dog, the garden, and everything, and I also keep the books for Dad's business."

"A little part-time job," sneered Cindy. "Grandma Ursula raised five children all by herself and worked full time in the department store."

When Cindy left for school, Linnea sat down with a cup of coffee. Cindy's comment about a part-time job stung. She spent half of her weekends on this task. Carl walked into the living room and, seeing her with a cup of coffee, remarked that he wished he had that kind of free time. He gave her a long list of errands and then complained that the lunch she made for him was uninspired. Linnea had packed Carl a turkey sandwich with an apple and some chips on the side.

"Yes, I know, your mother always prepared the most surprising, delicious lunches, never the same things two days in a row," growled Linnea.

When Carl left, Linnea made herself a second cup of coffee, looked at the chore list, crumpled it into a ball, and stuffed it into her purse.

"Firefighting is not a woman's job? Does he even know his daughter?" she said to herself, grabbed her purse, and walked over to the town's fire station.

"What would it take to become a firefighter?" she asked.

The man she spoke to looked her up and down and grinned.

"Aren't you a bit too old for that, Lady?"

"No, really, what would it take?"

"You can volunteer with us for a while, and if it works out, you can take EMT classes. There are exams to pass, and you must be in top-fit condition."

The man paused, then he snickered and said, "Forget it, Lady."

"Pfff," said Linnea and walked to the nearest gym, where she hired a personal trainer.

"I need to be in top shape," she said. "Train me without pity."

The trainer, Tammy, was young, maybe twenty if that. She had a trim body, short brown hair, and an infectious smile.

"I'll get you in the best shape ever," she said. "And we'll get rid of these extra pounds, too."

"Yeah, right," grumbled Linnea. "I've tried that for the past nine years."

Those ten extra pounds were a leftover from having Cindy. The little love handles wouldn't have been so bad, except that Ursula kept pointing them out every chance she got.

Just yesterday, when Linnea ladled stew into everyone's bowls, Ursula cocked an eyebrow and suggested, "Maybe, Sweetie, half a portion would do for you? You know, no man likes to be married to a whale."

On the first day of training, Tammy made Linnea jump rope and stretch thick rubber bands. The jump roping did not go so well; Linnea got her feet tangled up with the rope and hit the ground. The next day, her right knee was swollen and sore.

Linnea got herself a knee brace and went back to the gym. Tammy started with biceps curls. Linnea lifted five pounds without trouble.

"Not too bad for a middle aged lady," she grinned.

Tammy took the five-pound weights away and handed Linnea some ten-pounders.

"Ten reps," said Tammy.

Ten reps were way too many. Linnea's arms threatened to fall off. She was breathing hard and sweating.

"Done," gasped Linnea after the tenth, painful lift.

Tammy nodded and handed her a fifteen-pound weight. Linnea's arms trembled. She strained and groaned and moved the weight over the horizontal, then her muscles failed, and the weight clattered on the ground, hitting her big toe.

"Do you get any satisfaction from torturing people?" yelled Linnea, surprised that she had enough breath left to yell.

"I've done worse," said Tammy, then she added, "Now your triceps."

Linnea clenched her teeth and picked up the dumbbells.

"Now let's see about those abdominals," said Tammy when Linnea finished the triceps exercises, yelping and wincing like an injured puppy.

Linnea went to the gym every day. She pushed, pulled, climbed, and contorted herself on thin little mats on the floor, all the while sweating, groaning, and aching. Tammy kept track of her progress and when Linnea could do a fifteen-pound biceps curl without swearing, Tammy invited Linnea for a banana split.

The exercise Linnea hated most was those God-forsaken one-legged Romanian deadlift. Tammy made her stand on one leg, holding the other leg horizontally behind her and bending down at the hip to lower a heavy weight to the ground. Linnea thought that she looked like a plastic drinking flamingo; all she needed was a pink suit.

"Older women need balance training to avoid falls," said Tammy.

"I am not THAT old," protested Linnea while she bent down with the weight and promptly lost her balance.

Once her knee healed, Linnea went jogging in the park and swimming in the town's pool.

Her husband did not notice a thing. The house was clean, the dinner was cooked, the chores were done, and the books were kept.

Ursula, on the other hand, noticed everything and was not sparing with her comments.

"How wonderful that you are finally putting a little effort into your appearance," she commented sweetly. "Now, if you could do something about that greasy hair."

One day, Linnea could not find her gym bag. She looked all over the house and finally retrieved it from the outside garbage can. Linnea marched up the stairs to confront her mother-in-law. Ursula smiled serenely and said that something as smelly as this gym bag had no business being in her house.

"YOUR house?" Linnea huffed, then she turned around, slammed the door, and threw the bag with everything in it in the washing machine.

After three months of grueling training, Linnea was in the best shape of her life, trim and full of energy. It was Sunday evening, and she was in a good mood. She retrieved two bottles of beer from the refrigerator and sat down with her husband.

"I am going to volunteer for the firefighters," she announced. "You will need to help around the house. Maybe you could cook dinner on those days when I am late?"

Her husband's jaw fell open as he stared at his wife.

"Have you lost your mind? I don't know how to make dinner. And anyway, that's your job."

"Not anymore," Linnea said. "Get take-out if you don't want to cook. Or ask your mother to do it."

The next day, Linnea reported to the fire station to volunteer. She had applied makeup and put her freshly washed hair in a neat ponytail.

Seven firefighters were sitting in the team room, drinking coffee and playing cards. Linnea noticed that they were all on the small side. The chief, a white-haired man with a beard, was the tallest of the bunch and could not have measured more than five feet.

The chief laughed, "Lady, this is a man's job."

"Says who?" Linnea asked. "Try me."

The chief and two of the men whispered to each other, and then the chief said, "OK, Lady, you can make yourself useful around here. Let's start with some coffee."

Linnea made coffee for the seven firefighters; then, she was sent to clean the little kitchen and sweep the team room.

"Done," Linnea said. "Now what? Don't I need a uniform?"

The youngest firefighter, a youth with very large ears and the only one among the men who did not have a beard, gave Linnea one of his uniforms. Linnea sat down with needles and thread to make it fit, and while she was at it, she also fixed missing buttons and tears on the uniforms of the other guys.

The next day, Linnea returned to the fire station, made coffee, and chatted with the men.

Then, an emergency call came in.

"Stay behind," the chief said to Linnea.

"I have had CPR training," Linnea said while she climbed on the truck. "I know how to behave in an emergency."

This thing about CPR training was actually an understatement. Linnea was a licensed nurse, but she had not worked in ten years and felt self-conscious about it.

"Then stay out of the way," the chief snapped because there was no time to argue.

The truck took off, sirens blaring, Linnea holding on for dear life. Her heart was racing. The call was about a house fire. Smoke billowed out of the kitchen window. Already, the fire licked at the siding, and a dry bush next to the house was aflame.

The firefighters ran to connect their hose with the fire hydrant while Linnea looked on from the sidewalk, where the chief had put her with stern orders to stay put.

Three men held the heavy hose and trained it on the house. Then, the remaining four men put on their protective gear and ran into the house to look for survivors. They carried out an elderly man and his wife. Linnea took one look at the man who was coughing and wheezing and noted the tell-tale drooping of the left side of his face.

"I think he's had a stroke," she said. "We must get him to the stroke unit as quickly as possible. It's farther away than the town hospital, but there is only a three-hour window in which to reverse a stroke."

The Chief raised his eyebrows, paused for a moment, and then said, "Yes, Ma'am."

The firefighters put oxygen masks on the two patients and rushed them to the regional stroke unit.

From that day on, Linnea always went with the firefighters. They taught her how to hold the heavy hose. Linnea learned where to point the water, how to don safety equipment, and the best way to transport an injured person.

Four weeks after Linnea's first fire, the firefighters received a gift basket and a bouquet of roses from the elderly couple whom they had saved.

"I think those should be yours," said the Chief as he handed the bouquet to Linnea.

Most days, Linnea managed to be home in time to make dinner, but one afternoon, the fire crew was busy, and the chief asked Linnea to stay a bit longer.

Linnea called home and pleaded with Ursula, "Please, Ursula, would you make dinner tonight? There is no way I can be home in time, and Carl says your dinners are the best in the world."

Ursula gladly agreed, and when Linnea came home, she found Carl and Cindy as happy as well-fed babies. Ursula had made pot roast with potato dumplings, gravy with red wine, and tiny peas in butter sauce. The dessert was raspberry cheesecake.

Unfortunately, there were no leftovers for Linnea, so she had a bologna sandwich. The kitchen was piled with dirty dishes, there were food smudges on all counters, and the stove was caked with some half-burned residue. The garbage can was overflowing and there were sticky puddles on the kitchen floor. Ursula declared that she had cooked, and the clean-up, therefore, was entirely Linnea's job.

The next time Linnea was late, Ursula grumbled but agreed to make some spaghetti with tomato sauce. The spaghetti was a little overcooked, but nobody complained. The third time, Ursula made turkey sandwiches on stale bread. The fourth time, she ordered pizza delivery.

One day, the firefighters were called to a fire in an abandoned building. The house was full of flammable clutter, so the fire spread quickly. While the men were connecting the hoses, Linnea thought she heard a whimpering nearby. She circled the house, and there, cowering under the porch, was a frightened little dog. Linnea called to it, sweet-talked it, and pleaded with it, but the pup was too scared to crawl out from its hiding place. The house was now an inferno of flames.

"Come here, little doggie," Linnea yelled, in tears because she feared that the house was about to collapse. The dog yelped but stayed where it was. So, Linnea crouched down in the dirt, crawled under the porch, and grabbed the dog. She made it out just in time before the porch went up in flames.

When she got home, her husband was enraged.

"I didn't marry a firefighter," he said. "I married a stay-at-home mom."

"Not so," said Linnea. "When I married you, we agreed that I would stay home until Cindy was ready for school. We are WAY past this time."

"By the way, my Mom left this morning," growled Carl.

"Really?"

"Yes, she said she hadn't come to pick up your slack."

"Well, you and Cindy both need to help more."

"Can you still do the bookkeeping?" asked Carl.

At that moment, Cindy poked her head through the door and said, "And drive me to kickboxing?"

"Let's make a plan," said Linnea, then turned to Cindy. "You can help me study for the EMT exams. And when you are older, you can volunteer, too."

Cindy shrugged, "I changed my mind. I want to be a fighter pilot."

*"So did Cindy become a fighter pilot?" asked Fanny.*

*"No, she changed her mind about five more times. In the end, she became an ocean explorer, and she is currently diving with dolphins."*

*****

*Fanny, as much as she liked to argue with Michael, did take his advice ("this one time") and got into medical school. There, the Angel of Death was Fanny's much-too-frequent companion. He hung around so much that he got on Fanny's nerves.*

*One evening, she went to a picnic on the lawn in front of the dormitory, having some beer with a cute boy. She was very much in the mood for a kiss or two when the angel appeared next to her on the blanket, frowning and shaking his head. Luckily, the young man could not see Michael, and Fanny was not drunk enough to point out that there was an angel on her blanket.*

*"WHAT do you want?" she hissed at the angel under her breath.*

*"That guy is no good," Michael whispered. "He'll get you pregnant and then disappear. He has already done that to two other girls."*

*"Spoilsport," Fanny grumbled, but she got up and left the party without getting a single kiss.*

*In the evening, Michael appeared in Fanny's dorm room and asked, "Are you OK?"*

*"I'll NEVER have a boyfriend," Fanny muttered.*

*Then she smiled, "Can you tell me a love story?"*

*"Of course," Michael said.*

# Chapter Twenty-Seven

# The Woman Who Wanted Her Husband Back

There once was a woman named Mira, who was married to a man whom she loved more than her life. She adored him so much that she did everything she could think of to make him happy. She cooked him the most delightful meals, kept the house sparkling clean, and always told her husband that he was the most amazing man under the sun.

Mira was a petite woman with auburn hair, green eyes, and a few freckles on her nose. She was proud of her tiny waist and shapely legs. Mira wore tight-fitting skirts and high heels even when she was vacuuming the house. She never let her husband see her without makeup.

One day, the husband came home from work and asked Mira to sit down. He rummaged through his briefcase and pulled out a stack of papers, which he gave to his wife.

Mira read the first line and gasped, "You are divorcing me? Have I not been an exemplary wife to you? How can you do that to me?"

"I found a woman who is both younger and prettier than you," said the man. "I hope you won't take this too hard. After all, a man must look out for himself."

The man left, saying that a lawyer would contact Mira about splitting up their possessions. He pointed out that the house was in his name and would be his alone, so he wanted her to move out within a week. Then he added that Mira could take the kitchen utensils if she liked.

Mira was too stunned to even cry. She packed a few clothes and walked to the house of her girlfriend, Anja, who lived next door.

"Can I stay with you for a while?" asked Mira. "My husband has left me, and he is kicking me out of our home."

In the days that followed, Mira cried and raged while Anja held her in her arms and tried to console her.

In many ways, Anja was Mira's opposite: she was a solidly built woman who kept her brown hair in a no-nonsense long braid and usually wore sneakers, jeans, and checkered shirts. Anja loved to work in her garden and often sang to herself - loudly.

She had never married, saying that "men just weren't her thing."

When all her consoling did not cheer Mira up, Anja said, "I know a witch who lives on the other side of town. She may have a spell or two for you."

So, Mira went to see the witch. The witch lived in an ordinary house, except that it was painted all black, and the front door was as red as blood. The house had a messy little garden consisting mostly of various herbs and weeds.

As Mira knocked at the blood-red door, her heart thumped in her chest, and her brow was covered in pearls of sweat. She had expected the witch to be an ugly old hag with a crooked nose and most of her teeth missing. Instead, the witch who opened the door was a young woman, buxom and dressed in a loose, flowery gown. Her feet were bare and had purple nail polish. She had black hair that she wore in elaborate braids, held in place by clips with tiger eye stones.

The witch scrutinized Mira, and before Mira could utter a word, the witch said, "Tsk, tsk. Have you been left by your no-good husband? And now you want revenge?"

"Not revenge," cried Mira. "I love him. No harm shall befall him. I just want him back."

"Hmmm," said the witch. "Aren't you afraid he'll just start cheating again?"

"He can cheat all he wants," said Mira. "I am not the jealous type. I just want him back in my house and in my bed."

"Is he that good in bed?" asked the witch, raising her eyebrows.

"Actually not," admitted Mira. "There is little fun for me in it. If he gives me a minute once a year, it's a lot."

"So then, does he spoil you with gifts and fancy vacations?"

"No, he doesn't do that either. The last time he remembered my birthday was ages ago, and he always says we do not have money for vacations."

The witch frowned.

"So, he is poor?"

"Not really. He drives fancy cars and buys himself designer suits, but he never lets me see his bank statements."

"You need a lawyer, not a witch," grumbled the witch.

"I just want him back!" yelled Mira, then she added, "A woman is nothing without a man."

"Fine," said the witch, shrugging her shoulders.

She rummaged among some items on the top shelf in her living room and retrieved a small brown vial.

"This is a love potion. Sprinkle three drops in his coffee, and he will fall madly in love with the first woman he sees. Make sure it's you he sees."

Mira took the vial and invited her husband over to Anja's house to discuss the divorce. She baked his favorite cake and made marvelous coffee with chocolate flavor and whipped cream on top.

When her husband arrived, she poured him a cup of coffee and, when he didn't look, added three drops from the vial.

Unfortunately, just then, she had a terrible stomach cramp and needed to go to the bathroom. While she was busy there, the doorbell rang.

"I'll get it," yelled her husband.

"Noooo," cried Mira, but she was too late. A young delivery girl stood in the doorway, and her husband gazed at her with wide eyes. A droplet of drool formed in the corner of his mouth.

The next day, Mira asked Anja to come with her to see the witch again and report the mishap.

"Unfortunately, love potions can only be used once on each human man," said the witch, shaking her head. "You are out of luck."

"Is there no other way?" cried Mira. "I want him back!"

Anja shook her head. "I sure don't understand why."

The witch looked from Mira to Anja and back, then she went to retrieve her crystal ball.

"Allow me a minute," she said while she whispered to the ball, which made strange howling noises and flickered in ghostly lights.

Finally, the witch cackled and said, "There is another way, but it is long and arduous, and you two have to do it together."

The witch sat down at her desk and scribbled a list of ingredients and the places where they could be found.

"Get me all of the items on the list before the end of the year, and we will see what we will see," she said.

"I'll be glad to come with you, Mira," said Anja. "I sure could use a vacation."

So, the two set off to collect herbs with strange names and pungent aromas. Their first stop was in Mumbai, India. The friends walked across the crowded marketplace and looked at all the stalls with exotic foods and spices. Anja bought a necklace made of seashells and put it around Mira's neck.

For the first time in months, Mira smiled. She placed a little kiss on her friend's cheek, which made Anja blush.

One item on the witch's list was a rare curry powder. Mira asked many shopkeepers, but nobody had ever heard of that spice.

"You have to flirt with them," said Anja. "Like this."

Anja sidled up to one of the shopkeepers and whispered the name of the spice in the man's ear, all the while running her hand across his broad chest. The man may have blushed, but his skin was so dark that Mira could not tell. He walked into the back of his shop and returned with a little bag of yellow powder.

"Are you free tonight?" he asked Anja.

"Some other night, maybe," said Anja and smiled.

"Wow," said Mira. "I have to try that."

The next item on the list was a herb by the name of Shatavari. Mira tried sidling and ear whispering, but the shopkeeper swatted her away. He rummaged in a drawer and gave her a plant whose white flowers had a strong aroma of bitter almonds.

"I don't think you need Shatavari," the shopkeeper grumbled.

"It's an aphrodisiac for women," giggled Anja.

That night, the two women shared a single bed in a sweltering hotel room. It was too hot for even a nightgown. The sound of street music wafted through their open window. They were both exhausted and fell asleep in each other's arms.

"Where to now?" asked Mira when morning broke.

"The Himalayas," said Anja. "Your witch wants us to get a green herb called Brahmi."

"The Himalayas?" groaned Mira. "Can't we get Brahmi in one of the markets here?"

"No, it has to be Himalayan Brahmi, freshly harvested by a monk, and it says we need to make the last mile of the trip on foot."

"Fine," sputtered Mira, and so the two friends set out for a trip to Mount Everest.

The women took a plane, then a rickety train, and finally an even more decrepit bus and deboarded at the last stop. They had arrived at the foot of the majestic mountain.

"That's for experienced mountaineers," Mira stuttered when she saw the cloud-covered peak.

"Don't worry," said Anja. We'll only have to hike for a mile to the nearest monastery."

A friendly villager pointed out the hiking trail that wound itself up the mountainside. It was noon, so the two friends set out right away.

"A mile won't take very long," said Anja. "We will sleep in the monastery tonight."

The women trudged along the path, and all was well until they encountered a roadblock. A muddy avalanche had buried the trail, making any further progress impossible.

"Maybe we should return to the village," said Anja.

"No, we can walk around the avalanche," objected Mira. "If we don't make it to the monastery, we won't get the Brahmi, and all our travels will have been for naught."

So, the women cut into the woods next to the buried path, trying to find a way around the avalanche. The ground was slippery, and the vegetation was dense, so they made little headway. Before long, they came across a deep ravine and had to turn around. The sun hid behind a thick layer of clouds, and soon, the two women lost all sense of direction. Then, Mira stumbled and slid into a ditch. Anja tried to help her up, but Mira's foot would not carry her weight. Anja heaved and pulled with all her strength until she had hauled Mira out of the ditch, but there was no way Mira could go any further.

"Go back to the village," said Mira. "Get me some help. I will be OK waiting for you here."

"No way," said Anja. "We'll spend the night in the woods together, and by tomorrow, let's hope that you can hobble a little."

The two friends huddled up under the canopy of a large cedar tree and shared what little food they had, mostly trail mix and a few mandarin oranges. Fortunately, Anja found a small brook nearby, so she filled their water bottles. They tried to make a campfire, but the wood was wet and would not catch fire.

Halfway through the night, the two women woke up with a start. There was a rustling in the bushes, and Mira thought she saw glowing eyes. Nothing attacked them, though, and eventually, they both fell asleep again. When dawn broke, Mira and Anja woke up to a strange sight. A very tall, shaggy man was busying himself with a campfire. He had enormous, bare feet and was clothed in animal furs. The man grunted something and pulled a charcoaled squirrel out of the fire. He tore it into three pieces and offered some to the two women.

"It's a Yeti," whispered Anja.

"Rumtatwa," growled the Yeti.

"We need to get to the monastery," said Mira.

"Rumtatwa?"

Anja showed the Yeti a cell phone picture of the monastery where they were headed. Then she pointed to Mira's leg and made a limping motion. The Yeti smiled, nodded, and grunted, and then he picked Mira up in his strong arms. He slung her over his shoulder like a bag of potatoes and stomped ahead through the thicket, with Anja following in his footsteps. Before long, they reached a stream, and behind it, they saw a sprawling building with gardens and fields.

"The monastery!" exclaimed Mira.

The Yeti gestured for Anja to wait while he carried Mira across the stream. Then he returned to do the same thing for Anja.

"Thank you, thank you," cried Mira.

"Rumtatwa," said Anja, and the Yeti gave her a wide grin.

"Rumtatwa," he said, turned around, and disappeared into the woods.

The monks took the two women in and treated Mira's sprained ankle with potions and salves. Mira and Anja shared a small room that had only one bed. The bed was hard and narrow, but it had heavenly-clean, white sheets and a single warm blanket. In the cool air of the Himalayas, the two women cuddled up under the blanket to keep each other warm.

At the crack of dawn, a young monk dressed in a red robe poked his head through the door and motioned for the women to follow him. Mira limped and leaned heavily on Anja. The monk led his guests to the colorful prayer room, where the monks were already chanting and beating a variety of drums and cymbals. Then, the sound of a conch announced breakfast time. The monks served roasted barley flour mixed with butter tea.

Next were chores; Anja helped out in the garden, and Mira was given long grasses to weave traditional baskets. She did her best, but the baskets came out uneven and misshapen, no matter how hard she tried. The head monk smiled politely and brought her more grass. Mira thought that he said something about patience and practice. She kept weaving until her fingers bled. The head monk inspected her blood-stained baskets and frowned.

"Perfection is not a worthy goal," he said, and took away her supply of grass.

Slowly, Mira's ankle healed, and when she was ready to leave, the head monk supplied the women with a sample of freshly harvested Brahmi. Then, the monks escorted Mira and Anja to the village so that they would not get lost again.

"What's next on our list?" asked Mira.

"Only one more item," said Anja. "We are supposed to get a few chocolates from the Maison Lenôtre in Paris."

"That's strange!" exclaimed Mira.

"It gets stranger. We are both supposed to eat one of the chocolates each, but only one. Under no circumstances are we allowed to eat more than one."

Mira and Anja took a plane to Paris and decided to spend two days in the City of Love. They ambled along the Champs-Élysées, visited the Palais de Versailles, and fed the pigeons at the shore of the Seine. Mira had their portrait sketched by one of the artists among the bouquinistes. In the evening, they gawked at the brightly lit Tour d'Eiffel. The friends had dinner in a fine restaurant, where the tables were set with white tablecloths, and the wine came in dusty, old bottles.

The next morning, Mira and Anja set out to visit the chocolate maker. The scent in the small store was intoxicating. There were hundreds of fancy sweets, some made with marzipan, some with hazelnut cream, and there were chocolate-covered raspberries and candy that looked like tree bark. The two women picked some praline cubes inscribed with the chocolatier's name, "Lenôtre."

"Let's have some coffee," said Anja.

Mira and Anja found a little street café, and there, they each had their one prescribed piece of chocolate. It was heavenly. The chocolate melted on their tongues and produced an aroma so rich and so subtle that the friends thought themselves in paradise.

Alas, no human being can eat only one of these chocolates. When the women had finished the whole bag of chocolates, they looked at each other in dismay.

"We have failed," cried Anja. "Now, you will never get your husband back."

"Who cares," sobbed Mira. "I have you. You are better than ten husbands to me."

When the two women arrived back home, they went to the witch's house to confess their failure.

The witch laughed when she heard about the chocolate disaster.

"Too bad," she said. "I had hoped you'd bring me at least one."

Then, she collected the herbs, sniffing the Shatavari with the air of a connoisseur.

"Come on in," said the witch and led Mira and Anja into a small, hidden room. Heavy red curtains covered the windows. The only light came from two candles that flickered next to the fireplace. There was a powerful scent of incense. The witch made the two women kneel on the soft carpet in front of the crystal ball. She struck a gong and chanted an incantation.

"You have passed your test," the witch intoned. "In the eyes of the coven, you are now joined together as one."

"What?" asked Mira and Anja.

"Unless you don't want to?" said the witch, raising her eyebrows.

Anja and Mira looked at each other, then Mira took Anja's hand and said, "I do."

"Me, too," said Anja.

*"That WAS a great love story," Fanny said. "How did it end for Mira's husband?"*

*"Well, Mira got the best lawyer, a member of the witch's coven. The lawyer placed a curse on the husband, and Mira ended up with the house, lots of alimony, and the car. The husband's new girlfriend left him because the man was insanely infatuated with the delivery girl, and the delivery girl, who was only sixteen, took him to court for harassment. It was a thing of beauty."*

*****

*Fanny scraped by in medical school. She had a scholarship, and Grandma helped, but she still needed some extra money, so she worked night shifts at the University Hospital. Mostly, she answered call bells and passed out bedpans.*

*One night, she was sent to help with the care of a very ill woman who was oozing blood from all orifices. Fanny could not change the bed linens as fast as the woman soiled them. The stench was unbearable. Then, she saw the Angel of Death standing next to her patient.*

*"YOU again," Fanny grumbled. "She is only forty; she has three children at home."*

*"I am not here for her," the angel said. "I was just checking how you were holding up."*

*Fanny snorted and gave the woman another fresh sheet for a blanket.*

*"I am OK," she said. "This was your idea, me becoming a doctor. Do you have any more glorious ideas, Godfather Death?"*

*The angel shrugged, looking embarrassed.*

He was about to disappear when he changed his mind and said, "You can still write, Fanny. These life experiences will give you some grist for the mill. Without those, what would you write about?"

Fanny sighed and said, "Go away," but she could not quite suppress a smile. "See me tonight at my dorm. I want to hear another story."

"I know a story about a vampire who was allergic to blood," Michael said with a grin.

"YES!" Fanny exclaimed. "Let's hear it."

"It's a pretty grim story," Michael cautioned. "But it's also funny."

"Funny and grim seem to go together with you," Fanny said.

# Chapter Twenty-Eight

# The Vampire Who Was Allergic to Blood

Little Danny was five when he was turned into a vampire. The boy and his parents were taking a late afternoon stroll in the park. The trees stood bare and skeletal against the darkening sky. The brown leaves on the grass had been disintegrating for some time, and some were as fragile as butterfly wings, ghostly with their veins laid bare.

Danny was a stout little boy, blonde-haired and stubby-nosed. He kicked up some leaves with his boots, then gathered an armful of wet foliage and let it rain over his head. The leaves smelled of mushrooms and dirt.

"I am a wood elf," yelled Danny, dancing about with leaves in his hair.

His parents laughed at the sight, but suddenly, they became silent. Something rustled in the shrubs, there was a low growling, and then dark figures emerged from the shadows. Before the parents could scream, the vampires were all over them. One of the monsters pounced on Danny's mother and sank his teeth into her neck. While he drained the woman, the other three vampires seized Danny's father and took turns drinking from his jugular. The man screamed and pleaded for mercy as he was passed from one vampire to the next. When they were finished with Danny's father, they dropped his lifeless body to the ground and sniffed the air. They quickly found little Danny, who was hiding in a pile of leaves. One of the vampires grabbed the squirming kid and smiled at him with pointy teeth.

"How about a little treat for you, young man?" he asked. "I have immortality for you if you like?"

The vampire punctured the boy's neck gently with the tips of his fangs, causing only the tiniest marks. Danny wiggled and screamed while the vampire slurped up some of the boy's blood.

"Now it's your turn, little fellow!" said the vampire and nicked his own wrist with his teeth. He put the bleeding wound against Danny's mouth, making the boy swallow some of his blood.

A minute later, the child broke out in hives. His face turned beet-red, and he wheezed like an old man. The vampire wrinkled his nose in disgust and dropped the boy to the ground.

"Not every transformation succeeds," the vampire grumbled. He and his followers walked away.

The ground was cold and wet, and the last of the daylight had faded. The trees cast eerie, swaying shadows by the light of the moon.

Danny shivered and whimpered to himself. He crawled to his mother's dead body and snuggled against her cold chest. After what felt like an interminable time, a man and a woman, who both seemed to be in their twenties, walked onto the scene.

The woman bent over the boy's dead mother and sniffed. Danny's eyes widened when he noticed the woman's long fangs.

"Go away," he tried to yell, but he could only squeak.

"Hi there, little man," said the woman, smiling sweetly. "I am Marietta. Don't be afraid of us. We won't hurt you."

Marietta had lustrous black hair, a lithe figure, and warm brown eyes. Her husband, Bonifacius, was quite the opposite of her, with a stocky build, blue eyes, and a blonde crew cut. Marietta cradled little Danny while her husband shook his head and frowned.

"I never had a child," Marietta mused. "Bonifacius, do you think…?"

"No!" said Bonifacius.

"Please?" Marietta said. "Please, can we keep him?"

"He will never look any older than five," her husband muttered. "How on Earth will he make it in this world?"

"We'll just have to move every few years," Marietta said. "So that the neighbors don't notice that we have a forever-five-year-old."

Bonifacius grumbled something about never winning any arguments with Marietta, picked up the child, and carried him to their home. Danny passed out in Bonifacius' arms and slept all night and all day. When he finally woke up, he was ravenous.

"Bonifacius," yelled Marietta. "Get me some of our freshest blood. The boy is awake."

Marietta spooned a little blood from a plastic pouch into Danny's mouth. The boy coughed, sputtered, and broke out in hives. He could barely breathe, and he scratched himself furiously. Marietta sponged him down with cold water and cradled him in her arms until the little boy's wheezing subsided.

"Go, get some O Rh-negative from the blood bank," Marietta told her husband. "That's the least allergenic blood type."

Bonifacius returned an hour later, carrying a cooler with the precious blood. Marietta squirted a drop of O Rh-negative blood on a spoon and put it on Danny's lips. But, sure enough, there were the hives and the wheezing again.

"Try animal blood," Marietta suggested.

Bonifacius nodded, mumbled, "Yes, dear," and disappeared into the night.

Bonifacius found a nearby veterinary surgery. None of the surveillance cameras recorded him, and Bonifacius was well-practiced in making no noise and leaving no traces.

It was midnight, and at first, the animal clinic was quiet. Bonifacius tiptoed from room to room until he found a dozen caged dogs kept overnight. Most wore cones to keep them from chewing off their stitches. The dogs started a ruckus of barking and howling, but Bonifacius gave every dog a treat, and then he took a miniature schnauzer out of its kennel. He laid it down on the examination bench, stroking and whispering to it, and expertly removed a few milliliters of the dog's blood with a syringe.

"There, there," Bonifacius said, giving the dog another treat. By now, the dogs had stopped barking because, obviously, this stranger was a source of goodies. Bonifacius collected five more syringes of blood and proceeded to the cat room.

The cats were unwilling to donate blood, treat or no treat. They hissed and scratched, and one bit Bonifacius.

"OUCH!" Bonifacius exclaimed. "You are lucky if I don't drink you empty!"

He found a sedative in the medicine cabinet, injected the feisty cat with it, and when it passed out, he collected a syringe full of its blood.

By the time Bonifacius came home, little Danny was so exhausted and limp that he could barely open his mouth. Unfortunately, the dog blood made him vomit, and the cat blood put him to sleep.

"Can a vampire die from starvation?" Bonifacius asked.

"I don't think so," Marietta mused. "After all, we ARE already dead. But I suppose if he doesn't get any blood, he will be weak and lethargic for the rest of his existence."

"Maybe we should put him out of his misery," Bonifacius said, glancing at the stake that leaned against the living room wall.

Little Danny was suddenly wide awake and withdrew into a corner of the room, howling.

Marietta bared her teeth and growled at Bonifacius, who dropped the subject, muttering, "Yes, dear."

In the following weeks, Danny languished in his little bed, whimpering, famished, and calling for his parents. He was as pale as a bed sheet, and his eyes had sunken into his skull. Marietta tried to cheer him up by reading to him and buying him toys, but Danny was too weak to pay attention.

Bonifacius brought cow blood, sheep blood, rat blood, elephant blood (from the zoo), and even gorilla blood (from a research facility) – all this did was give Danny more rashes and hives. By now, Marietta was prepared for the hives - she had assembled a treasure trove of EpiPens. But when the gorilla's blood caused Danny to grow orange hair all over his face (in addition to hives and wheezing), she shook her head in defeat. Fortunately, the orange hair fell out after a few days.

Then, one day, as Danny tiredly leafed through a picture book, he gave himself a paper cut. He howled feebly, then he sucked on his finger to stop the bleeding.

When Marietta came into his room a little later to check on the child, she found a little boy with pink cheeks and sparkling eyes. The child hopped up and down on his bed, then he pretended to be an airplane and jumped right into Marietta's arms.

Marietta saw the bleeding paper cut and ran to get Bonifacius.

"No way," said Bonifacius. "It's a physical impossibility. Little Danny can't be nourished by his own blood."

"Well, the laws of nature don't really apply to us," said Marietta.

So, from now on, Danny gave himself a papercut every few days, and that kept him healthy and active. But this dribble of blood did nothing to quell his ravenous hunger. Sometimes, his hunger got so bad that he was shaking. He felt empty, hollow, too light, but it was useless, so he learned to live with his painfully rumbling stomach.

One day, Danny wanted to know how Marietta and Bonifacius had met. Marietta smiled and squeezed Bonifacius' hand.

"I was seventeen when I met Bonifacius," Marietta began. "That was over two hundred years ago when I was a scullery maid at the village inn. I had stepped in front of the building to take out the garbage when ... The brute who held me down bit my neck and drank and drank. I was half dead when he made me swallow some blood from a wound on his wrist."

Bonifacius nodded, "I was walking down the road nearby, and I smelled the blood. When I saw the vampire bend over Marietta, I jumped and tore into him. Then I pulled my stake from my coat and rammed it into the vampire's chest."

"Wait," said Danny. "Why did you carry a stake?"

"I never got along with the other vampires. When I was a new vampire, I killed people for food, but the other vampires killed for sport. I saw them massacre whole villages. One day, I found the bodies of my parents and my six brothers and sisters, all killed by vampires. After that, I became a vampire hunter."

Bonifacius continued his story, "I tried to help Marietta, but I was too late. Marietta, of course, did not realize that she had been turned."

"True," said Marietta. "I thought I was dying, so I smiled at Bonifacius and breathed, 'At least I will die in the arms of a man, not a monster.' And at that, my Bonifacius started to cry, sobbing, 'You are wrong on all counts. You will not die, and I am no man.'"

"And then?" asked Danny.

"Then Marietta passed out," said Bonifacius. "I picked her up in my arms and carried her to my home, a shack deep in the woods."

Bonifacius smiled at the memory. "I was very proud of my little home. I had built it with my own hands, painted it forest green, and placed some containers with flowers on the porch. I raised chickens and rabbits, which I sold on the marketplace - after draining their blood for my own use."

Bonifacius paused, lost in thought, "I was alone in the world, and the shack reminded me of the time when I was human.

"When I got home, I put Marietta into my bed and lit a roaring fire in my fireplace because freshly turned vampires always crave warmth. Then I sat next to Marietta, waiting for her to wake up. All the time, I thought that I should kill this beautiful girl. What life would she have as a vampire? But I just couldn't do it."

"You are a softy," chuckled Marietta. "When I came to, I was ravenous, so Bonifacius went to his kitchen and returned with a bowl of warm blood. The blood smelled so good, I wanted to gobble it down all at once, but it also disgusted me."

"I explained to her that it was chicken blood," said Bonifacius. "I had chopped off the heads of two chickens and drained them into a bowl."

"And that's when I realized what had happened to me," said Marietta. "I was a vampire."

"The thing that bothered Marietta most about being a vampire was that she thought she had lost her soul," said Bonifacius. "She yelled at me, 'Why didn't you kill me?' and she sobbed and prayed."

Marietta nodded. "Without a soul, there was no way I could go to Heaven."

Bonifacius continued, "I tried to reassure her. Vampires lose their souls the first time they kill a human for their blood. Marietta still had her soul, while I had lost mine many years ago."

"So, you are bound for hell?" asked Danny.

"I am bound for nothingness," said Bonifacius. "My soul was destroyed; there is nothing left in me to go to Heaven or Hell."

For a few moments, everybody was silent.

"I decided that I would never kill a person," said Marietta. "At first, I lived off chicken and rabbit blood. And later, Bonifacius got a job at the blood bank, and he always brought home some blood that was past its expiration date."

"So, how did you two get married?" Danny asked.

"We settled into a quiet routine," Marietta said. "Bonifacius provided animal blood for me. He bought me clothes and toiletries, but he was always shy and never touched me. I finally got tired of looking at his sad, longing eyes, which followed me wherever I went.

"'If you want to be with me,' I told him. 'You cannot kill people anymore.'"

"And what do you think Bonifacius said?" Marietta asked.

"Yes, dear," Danny replied.

"Exactly. So, I kissed Bonifacius on his lips, and we were married in the eyes of God."

Bonifacius smiled, "From that day on, I never again bit a human. Sometimes, I have cravings for fresh human blood, but I love Marietta more than I love a good meal."

Danny nodded. He knew what it was to have cravings. He was always starving, always craving blood, salivating at the sight of the blood that Marietta kept in their refrigerator.

The years passed. The family moved every two years so the neighbors would not wonder why the little boy next door never got older. Danny was home-schooled, and since he had nothing else to do, he devoured every bit of knowledge he could find on the Internet.

On his twentieth birthday, Danny made an announcement, "Mom and Dad, I am going to college."

Danny paused for emphasis, "Stanford. They have a great biotechnology program."

"Huh?" Bonifacius said. "What's biotechnology?"

"I want to bioengineer artificial blood. I'll make something I am not allergic to."

"Sweetheart, you look like you're five," Marietta said. "And you have no diploma from anywhere. And you can't be out and about in daylight."

"Pfff," Danny said. "I need your help, but I know I can pull this off."

Getting a fake diploma was the easiest part. Danny found some forgery experts by researching the dark web. In no time, he had an authentic-looking high school diploma from Venezuela, a Bachelor's diploma in natural sciences from the University of Zagreb, and a dozen glowing letters of recommendation.

"How much money do we have?" Marietta asked. "I hear Stanford is expensive."

"I don't know," said Bonifacius. "I haven't checked our savings account for at least a hundred years."

Bonifacius was three hundred and twenty-two years old and had lived a modest, secluded life. The nest egg he had started three hundred years ago had grown uninterrupted with compounding interest.

Bonifacius went to the bank pretending to be the young heir to his great-grandfather, Bonifacius Jones. Danny provided the necessary paperwork.

When Bonifacius returned from his bank run, he asked his family to sit down.

"Not enough?" Danny asked.

"Ten billion," Bonifacius said. "Is that enough?"

So, a few of Bonifacius's millions bought an endowment at the University of Stanford and an acceptance letter for Danny. The University agreed to waive its initial interview.

"And now?" Marietta fretted. "You still look five!"

"Dad will go to class for me. He looks twenty-two."

Bonifacius broke out in a sweat, "I know nothing about science. When I was turned, I was a blacksmith by day and a burglar by night. In my day, medicine was bloodletting and leeches."

"Not to worry," Danny said, producing some almost invisible earphones and a tiny microphone. "You wear these, and I'll tell you what to say."

Bonifacius' hands were shaking when he took the earphones and put them in his ears.

"This is a very bad idea," he said. "If I get exposed for what I am, the humans will hunt down and kill all three of us."

He looked at Marietta and said, "Promise you will run if I tell you?"

Marietta nodded. "I love you, my Bonifacius."

"Danny, my son," said Bonifacius. "I will do this for you even though I think this is utter folly."

Danny hugged his father and whispered, "Thank you, Dad."

Two weeks later, Bonifacius presented himself to the university under the name Danny Jones. Danny wanted a degree in his own name, which he realized was a bit of useless vanity. But still, he wanted to be Dr. Danny Jones one day.

Bonifacius sat through endless lectures that he did not understand at all while his son listened remotely. Bonifacius got permission to do his lab work at night (he claimed his mother was ill and needed him during the day), and he smuggled Danny with him into the lab. There, he watched as his son juggled petri dishes and DNA sequencers.

One night, as Danny was jubilant about a successful experiment, the lab door opened, and in came Danny's favorite teacher, Professor Olson. Professor Olson was a white-haired man with a gentle smile underneath a neat little mustache. He walked with a limp and used a cane.

"Danny?" the professor said, and both Bonifacius and Danny responded, "Yes?"

"So good of you to bring your son," Professor Olson said. "What's his name?"

"Igor," Danny said before his father could open his mouth.

"Nice to meet you, Igor." The professor paused, frowned, and shook his head. "Are you aware that this lab has surveillance cameras?"

"No," Bonifacius said hesitantly.

Danny would have blanched if he hadn't been completely pale already.

"I checked the tapes the other day," the professor continued. "Then I checked the recordings from several weeks back, and you were never here. Yet you produce amazing results."

Bonifacius stammered something, but his son sighed and said, "I think it's time for the truth, Dad. Professor Olson is a kind man and a marvelous professor. It's just wrong to deceive him."

Danny took the professor by the hand and walked with him to the mirror over the eye-washing station. The mirror showed the professor, but no one else; the professor's hand held on to nothing.

"The camera won't record us, Professor, just as the mirror does not reflect us," Danny said. "Please don't be scared. We are harmless vampires. My parents and I haven't had any fresh blood in ages."

The professor moved back and forth in front of the mirror, angling his head to try to see Bonifacius and his son reflected in it, and finally gave up. Then he walked to the surveillance camera and spooled the film back to watch the recording of the day.

"You aren't here," he said, shaking his head. "But you are here. And on the recording, the instruments are moving as if on their own. I had not noticed that at first."

"I am twenty-three years old," Danny said. "Unfortunately, I haven't aged since I was bitten, so I have to play this little charade."

"It can't be."

"Feel my pulse," Bonifacius said. "I haven't had one in over three hundred years."

"Where is that coffeemaker?" asked Olson, who badly needed some caffeine. "Would you like some? Or do you even drink coffee?"

Bonifacius smiled, "A cup of coffee would be lovely, Professor."

"So, why are you at Stanford?" Olson asked when the caffeine had restored some of his wits.

"I want to bioengineer plant-based, artificial blood," Danny said. "I am allergic to all the natural stuff."

"Aha." Olson paused. "I don't quite understand all the implications, but I'll help you, as long as you promise not to drink me."

"You'd just give me hives anyway," Danny said.

"Promised," Bonifacius said. "And my real name is Bonifacius. My son's name isn't Igor, it's Danny. Sorry."

The next day, Olson removed the surveillance cameras and destroyed the existing recordings. Every night, he and Danny pored over plant analogs of hemoglobin. They finally settled on soy because it was easy to grow.

"Soy makes leghemoglobin, close enough?"

"If we could get this into a yeast…"

"If it's in yeast, we can ferment it."

"And make hemoglobin beer?"

"Hemoglobin champagne!"

Danny worked like one possessed because work distracted him from his painfully growling stomach. After five years of research, three peer-reviewed research papers, and a doctorate in biotechnology, the blood substitute was ready. It smelled and looked like blood with just a little added fizz. The family was assembled in the laboratory. Bonifacius squeezed Marietta's hand, and Marietta had her EpiPens ready. Danny paced the lab like a caged tiger.

"Ready?" asked Olson.

"Ready."

Olson put some of the brew on a spoon and fed it to Danny. Danny swished it around in his mouth, savoring the taste.

"It's excellent," Danny exclaimed. "I would say dark chocolate and prune combined with a subtle earthiness."

Danny swallowed. There were no hives. He took another sip, and still there was no reaction. Then he grabbed the whole beaker and gulped down all its contents.

"And?" asked Olson.

"I have a weird sensation in my stomach," said Danny.

"What is it? Are you in pain? Is it burning you up from the inside?"

"No, no," said Danny, his eyes wide. "What I feel, I think, is the absence of hunger..."

Marietta, Bonifacius, Olson, and Danny celebrated in Olson's home. Olson lived alone in a modest house in Palo Alto. The street was quiet, lined with old trees, and the house was nestled in a well-kept little garden. The professor served vegan food, which Danny could tolerate. Of course, the food did not nourish the vampires; it went through them like water, but they appreciated the taste.

When the evening drew to a close, Olson asked, "And now?"

"Now, I'm starting a biotech company," Danny said. "We are so close. I think in a few years, we will produce plant-based blood on an industrial scale. And once we have that, I have an idea of how to commercialize it."

His father sighed, "How many millions do you need?"

"A few," Danny said, then he turned to Olson. "Would you like to join my new company as a scientific consultant, Professor?"

Professor Olson beamed and said, "I wouldn't miss it for the world."

Five years later, a large crowd assembled in the university auditorium. Cameras were not allowed. According to rumors, Danny Jones was extremely shy about having his picture taken. A sketch artist was allowed in, though.

Bonifacius, posing as Danny Jones and equipped with tiny earphones, was about to address the audience. Professor Olson sat in the front row, a bouquet of roses in his arms. Danny and Marietta listened from behind a curtain. They were holding champagne glasses that held a dark red, fizzing liquid.

"Ladies and gentlemen," began Bonifacius. "Let me introduce you to a miracle of bioengineering. This new invention will change the world. Mankind will finally live in peace with the rest of creation."

Behind the curtain, Danny and Marietta toasted each other with their champagne glasses. Danny's five-year-old face was glowing. The hemoglobin champagne was excellent vampire food, and it was also the most important ingredient of something else.

"Nobody thought it could be done, but we did," Bonifacius continued on the podium. "We made a plant-based meat that tastes like the real thing."

Bonifacius took a deep breath. "Ladies and gentlemen, meet the Meat that Isn't."

*"Wow," Fanny said. "Is this a true story?"*

*"You'd have to ask Danny Jones."*

*"Does Marietta still have her soul?"*

*"Yes, and so does Bonifacius. See, when a woman really loves a man, she shares a sliver of her soul with him. Marietta's sliver has grown in Bonifacius' chest for two hundred years. The funny thing is that he does not know that he has a soul."*

*"Do you have a soul, Michael?"*

*"No, Fanny. I was created without a soul. It's an irony. I deal with souls every day. It's what I do for a living. Yet, I can never have one myself."*

*"Would you ever want a soul?" Fanny asked.*

*Michael lowered his eyes and took a deep breath before he replied, "Yes, I would want a soul more than my life. But there is no point in longing for something one can't have."*

*"What would you want a soul for? Just so that your life doesn't end when you die?"*

*"No, that's not it. If I had a soul, I would have free will. Without a soul, I have to do what my mother asks me to do."*

*Michael looked down at his feet and clenched his fists, then he added, "I cannot deviate. I am but a tool in my mother's hands."*

*****

*One day, Fanny went to anatomy class, where she had to dissect a cadaver. The corpse smelled to high heavens of formalin, making Fanny's eyes and nose water. She had the job to lay bare the delicate arteries of the gut. Just as she sank her scalpel into the thin layer of skin that covered the blood vessels, the Angel of Death appeared next to the corpse and pointed out the dead man's large, cirrhotic liver.*

*"A drunk," the angel said. "He died a miserable death from liver failure."*

*Fanny was so distracted by what the angel said that she messed up the dissection.*

*"Are you doing this on purpose?" the anatomy assistant snarled at her.*

*"Go away," Fanny growled at Michael when the assistant was yelling at another student. "I can't concentrate with you around."*

*"It's not that you are grossed out, is it?" Michael asked.*

*"My Godfather is the Angel of Death. Nothing can gross ME out!"*

*"Hmmm," Michael said. "I know a story about a little girl who was never grossed out by anything. Want to hear it?'*

*"Tonight, with a bottle of wine or two," Fanny sighed.*

# Chapter Twenty-Nine

# The Girl Who Loved Creepy-Crawlies

Just one week after the wedding, Ginni's stepmother threw down the gauntlet. It was midmorning. Ginni, still in her pajamas, was stretched out on her bed, reading a book about ants and termites. Termites, Ginni learned, were more closely related to cockroaches than to ants. Termites had workers, winged males, queens, and soldiers. The soldiers had enormous jaws, so large and unwieldy that the workers had to feed them. Ginni pictured soldier termites lining up in a battle, opening and closing their jaws in anticipation.

It was a bright day. The sun poured a swath of warm light through the window. The bedroom walls, painted sky blue with pink cherry blossoms and little white clouds, sparkled in the sunlight.

As Ginni was engrossed in her book, her stepmother, Beatrice, stepped into Ginni's room, not bothering to knock. The open door created a draft, and the curtains fluttered with a gust of cold air. The sun hid behind a cloud, and all the colors in the room faded.

"My dear child," Beatrice said. "We need to talk."

"Now?" said Ginni, looking up from her book.

"Now," insisted Beatrice. "Clearly, your upbringing has been lacking. Not that I blame your father. He has more important things to do than correct an unkempt, ill-mannered urchin."

Ginni balled her fists and said nothing. She caught a glimpse of herself in her full-length mirror. She did look a bit scruffy; she had to admit. She was ten, a wiry kid with brown, unruly, shoulder-length hair. She had a wide mouth, green eyes, and two dimples on her cheeks.

"From now on, Genevieve," continued Beatrice. "You will wear suitable clothes and learn proper behavior."

"Genevieve" was Ginni's given name, but nobody called her that, nobody.

"What are suitable clothes?" Ginni asked, forcing herself to unclench her fists and her teeth.

Beatrice opened Ginni's closet and revealed a collection of long dresses and skirts, frilly blouses, polished black shoes, and various flowered sun hats. None of these things had been there the day before, and everything was brand new.

Ginni could not, for the life of her, imagine what she would do with all these clothes.

"The lady loves shopping," she thought.

The most remarkable thing about Beatrice was how slowly she moved, every gesture deliberate, like a tiger on the prowl. She had red hair piled on her head in an arrangement of hairspray and curls. Her eyes were more gray than blue, and they were cold.

"Where are my jeans?" Ginni asked.

"I directed Joseph to dispose of them," said Beatrice. "You don't need them anymore. You will stay inside except for supervised strolls around the castle."

"WHAT?!"

"You heard me."

Ginni had a vision of a Tarantula Hawk stinging Beatrice so that she would pass out in excruciating pain.

Ginni had been reading everything she could get her hands on about Tarantula Hawks. Those were not hawks; they were giant, red-winged wasps, and they had the most painful sting in the world. Tarantula Hawks hunted tarantulas, hence the name. When one of these wasps caught a tarantula, it paralyzed it with its venom and then laid a single egg into the spider's body. The larva grew by consuming the living host from the inside.

When Beatrice left the girl's room, Ginni let out a stifled scream.

She looked at her mother's framed portrait on the side of her bed. In the picture, Ginni's mother was smiling. She held baby Ginni, touching her cheek to the baby's fuzzy hair. Ginni realized how much she resembled her mother, down to the slight frame, the wide mouth, and the green eyes.

"Mommy," Ginni whispered. "I could use some help."

Ginni's mother did not respond, so Ginni went to find Joseph, the family's butler. He was in his forties, already balding, and wore a small, carefully trimmed mustache. He was dressed in his red and gold uniform with deep pockets that often held hidden small treats for Ginni.

"Hello, Miss Ginni," Joseph said, smiling warmly. "What's wrong?"

"Beatrice said you threw out all my outdoor clothes," Ginni muttered.

"Well, maybe," said Joseph. "And maybe I kept one or two outfits. It would be a shame to ruin all your new clothes when you climb a tree or roll in the mud, wouldn't it?"

Joseph opened a small closet hidden under the winding staircase, and inside it were all Ginni's play clothes, sneakers, and baseball caps.

"Yes!" exclaimed Gini and gave Joseph a bear hug.

Those clothes reminded Ginni of the day, years ago, when her father had taken her for her first hike on the estate. Ginni loved everything about Duggenham Manor: the castle that sat atop a hill overlooking a rocky ocean beach with small, white-crested waves, the old-growth forest, which was mostly used for hunting, and the stables, orchards, and fields.

On that first hike, Ginni's father showed Ginni a mossy rock and said, "Do you think you can turn over this rock, Sweetie?"

Ginni pushed and heaved, and then the rock rolled on its back. Where the rock had been, Ginni saw half a dozen little creatures wiggling in the moist dirt.

"This is an earthworm," said Ginni's father, pointing to a slimy, coiled-up thing.

"Eeeouw," said Ginni.

"Not eeeouw," said her father, picking up the earthworm. "Have a closer look."

Before Ginni knew it, she was holding the soft thing in the palm of her hand.

"See, not eeeouw at all," smiled her father.

From then on, Ginni was fascinated by insects. She also loved spiders and worms — everything creepy-crawly. Her father smiled at her obsession and called her his "Precious and Brave Lady Explorer." Ginni had an ant farm on her windowsill, and she had been begging her father to let her keep a tarantula. So far, this request was unsuccessful.

Ginni ripped herself from her memories and went to find her father in his study. He was poring over some paperwork, scowling, and shaking his head. He was about fifty, clean-shaven, still trim and athletic, but graying at his temples.

He looked up from his work and smiled at Ginni, "Yes, Sweetie?"

"Dad," stammered Ginni. "Beatrice just told me I can't go to the forest by myself anymore. Please, tell her to let me be."

Lord Duggenham shook his head, "Do what she says. Mothers know best."

"She is NOT my mother!" exclaimed Ginni.

"I expect you to treat her with the respect due to a lady," said Ginni's father.

"But Dad."

"There's no further need for discussion."

Ginni gasped and fled to her room.

"I am the Precious and Brave Lady Explorer," she reminded herself. "Lady explorers don't cry."

The following morning, Joseph knocked at Ginni's bedroom door and poked his head into her room. He held a brown paper bag with two sandwiches, a hard-boiled egg, and an apple.

"Peanut butter," he said, smiling. "Your favorite still, I believe?"

Joseph approached Ginni's window and muttered, "Look who's departing."

It was Beatrice leaving for an errand. Ginni grabbed the brown paper bag from Joseph and grinned.

Ginni waited a few minutes until she was sure her stepmother was gone. Then, she raced downstairs, put on jeans, T-shirts, and sneakers from the secret closet, ran outside, crossed the drawbridge, and disappeared into the woods.

She came home well after dinner, mud all over her shirt, and her hair covered with lichen and bark. Joseph had saved some chicken ragout for her in the warming oven.

In the following weeks, Ginni absconded to the woods on a daily basis. She slipped out in the early mornings, a shadow, unseen and unheard. Beatrice admonished Ginni. When that had no effect, she took her toys away, even the ant farm. When that failed to change Ginni's behavior, she confiscated Ginni's cell phone, and when that did not work either, she asked her husband to intervene.

Ginni's father summoned his daughter to his study. He sat behind his enormous, polished mahogany desk and frowned at his daughter. Ginni had a lump in her stomach. A year ago, her father would have greeted her with a hug. Ginni remembered how he always held her hand when they set out for a walk. He would ask her about her insect collection and make helpful suggestions. But ever since he had married Beatrice, there had been no more hugs, no forest hikes, no days at the beach, no talks about creepy crawlies.

"Beatrice has done much for you," Ginni's father said. "You must learn to be grateful."

Ginni looked down and didn't respond. The next day, she disappeared into the woods again.

Ginni never tired of the forest. One night, she crawled into a hollow tree, pretending to be hiding from kidnappers. Ginni loved the spooky old forest, especially when it was getting dark. The gnarly branches formed monstrous shapes in the evening mist, and Ginni's imagination added glowing eyes and claws.

Night had fallen when she set out to go home. She danced over tree roots and boulders by the light of the moon. She jumped over small creeks and raced across meadows. When she arrived at the castle, she was glowing with exertion. There was just nothing better than running to chase the nastiness of the world from her soul.

Ginni went straight to the kitchen, where Joseph had a plate of beef stew ready for her.

The next day, Ginni walked to a little pond known for its dragonflies. It was mating season, so Ginni sat down and held perfectly still. After about half an hour of waiting with bated breath, two iridescent blue creatures with long, lacy wings alighted on a small branch. They clung to each other and contorted their bodies to form the shape of a heart.

Ginni thought that she had to tell her dad about this - he would love to hear about dragonflies making love.

When she made it home to the castle, Ginni ran up to her father.

"Dad," said Ginni. "Guess what I found today."

"Ginni," said her father. "You know that you are not supposed to run in the woods. I don't want to hear about anything until you learn to obey your mother."

"But I saw two dragonflies making love..."

"Genevieve," said Beatrice. "We don't talk about this kind of thing in polite society."

On one warm summer day, Ginni spotted a bald-faced hornet's nest in the family's orchard. It looked like a cone made of papier-mâché with a small hole for an entrance at the tip. Black and yellow insects were flying in and out and crawling over the outer envelope of the nest to build more and more layers of papier-mâché.

Ginni researched hornets and found instructions on how to move a hornet's nest with the living insects in it.

The first thing Ginni needed was a beekeeper's suit. That was no problem; the friendly neighborhood beekeeper was happy to let her borrow his smallest suit. The next step would have been to put some sticky tape over the entrance hole of the nest and vacuum up any stray hornets with a hand-held vacuum cleaner. Then, Ginni would carry the nest with the insects in it over to her window and superglue it to the window frame.

Beatrice, however, saw Ginni donning the beekeeper suit, and that was the end of Ginni's plans to get her very own hornet swarm.

The hornets' nest was terrible enough, but it was the cat cadaver in Ginni's bedroom that finally drove Beatrice over the edge. Ginni kept it so that she could watch maggots hatch and turn into flies.

She had posted a sign on her bedroom door that said, "Enter at your own risk."

At Ginni's insistence, the servants were not allowed to clean Ginni's room, and even Joseph avoided it at all costs. But one day, Beatrice noticed a foul odor that seeped into the hallway from under Ginni's bedroom door. She opened the door, sniffing and gagging, and there on a plastic pad was a cat cadaver, half decomposed and swarming with maggots.

Beatrice screamed and ran down the stairs. In her hurry, she tripped, tumbled down the carpeted steps, and landed on the marble floor below. When she returned from the hospital, wearing a cast on her wrist, she summoned her husband. Ginni listened from behind the door.

"Ginni will become a social outcast the way this is going," said Beatrice. "She is as wild as a pony of the Camargue. She has no manners at all and no sense of what is proper and right. If we don't intervene now, it will be too late. She needs to attend a girls' boarding school."

Ginni's father wrinkled his brow and sputtered, "For the life of me, I cannot imagine Ginni in a boarding school."

"Arthur!" Beatrice said, her voice sharp enough to cut bread.

"As you said," Ginni's father said. "Mother knows best."

Ginni burst into the room and implored her father to please, please, not send her away, but he averted his eyes.

"This household needs peace," he said softly. "It will be for your own good."

Ginni noticed that her father's face was gray; he had a two-day-old beard, and his eyelids were drooping.

His eyes were so sad that Ginni swallowed and said, "Okay - if you are sure."

Ginni packed two suitcases, one with clothes and the other with her mother's picture, her favorite books about insects and spiders, some specimen jars, a magnifying glass, and tiny forceps.

And so, when fall painted the leaves in Ginni's beloved forest, Ginni wasn't there to look for stag beetles and fall webworms under the autumn leaves. She did not collect ladybugs, boxelder beetles, or pirate bugs.

Instead, she found herself in a stuffy classroom alongside a dozen other young ladies, all trying very hard to keep their backs straight and their faces pleasant. Everybody wore their school uniforms: plaid skirts, white blouses, white stockings, and black shoes. Ginni kicked off her shoes and wiggled her toes.

She looked around the classroom and noticed a life-sized portrait of the Queen on the back wall. There was a dusty blackboard and a collection of narrow, wooden desks that somebody must have appropriated from the torture chamber underneath London Tower.

Ginni studied the girls' nameplates, which had been arranged on their desks. Next to Ginni sat Louisa, who squirmed in her seat because her skirt was two sizes too small.

The teacher, Miss Butler, was different from what Ginni had expected. She was not old, did not wear tweed skirts, and did not have super-sized horn-rimmed glasses. Miss Butler was barely ten years older than Ginni, blonde, and full of infectious energy.

Still, the teacher had to follow her guidelines, so she wrote the prescribed curriculum for the next six months on the blackboard. It included learning graciousness, modesty, composure, and respect for elders.

After class, Ginni asked Miss Butler for permission to explore the land around the school.

"Of course, dear," said Miss Butler. "I'll come with you. A little evening stroll would be lovely."

The school was situated in a lush valley surrounded by vineyards, wheat fields, and apple orchards. The late summer sun bathed the landscape in its soft, golden light. Ginni skipped across a wild-flower-studded meadow where the crickets were singing to each other of everlasting love. The girl and the teacher followed a gurgling brook that led them into a small oak grove. Ginni crouched in front of a mossy rock and carefully turned it over. There were grubs, earthworms, and rollie-pollies, as expected, but Ginni also found a large beetle that looked as if it had been forged of a coppery metal chiseled with rows of tiny indentations.

"A necklace ground beetle," exclaimed Ginni.

Ginni and Miss Butler continued their walk and collected dozens of interesting creatures along the way. And then, there it was, an honest-to-God Tarantula Hawk. I sat on a little twig, its pitch-black abdomen curled under her, holding on to the sprig with all six limbs. Her translucent wings glowed orange in the afternoon sun. Ginni caught it with a small net, careful not to get stung.

"This wasp has the most horrible sting in the world," said Ginni. "It hunts tarantulas and lays its egg into the tarantula's paralyzed body."

"Does the larva eat the spider from within while the spider is alive?" whispered Miss Butler.

"Yes," said Ginni. "Isn't it awesome?"

Ginni had brought some of her specimen jars, so Miss Butler helped Ginni put their catch in separate glass containers. Then, they carried everything to the biology lab. For hours, Ginni and Miss Butler pored over various insect websites, classified the animals, and took pictures.

"Now we let them go," declared Miss Butler when they were done.

Ginni pushed her lower lip forward and blew a raspberry.

"All life deserves to be protected," said Miss Butler sternly.

Ginni took a deep breath and asked, "All life?"

"All life," confirmed Miss Butler.

"Even an ugly bug like me?"

"You are precious," Miss Butler said, ruffling Ginni's hair.

And so, the teacher and her student snuck into the night to free the creatures.

The next day, Ginni learned how to curtsey and use the correct fork for salad and fish. She learned to tilt her head just so and smile mysteriously. But after class, Ginni waited for Miss Butler outside the classroom, and off they went to look for more wildlife in the fields.

After a few weeks, Louisa noticed Ginni carrying a load of glass containers on a tray. Ginni was walking across the schoolyard to the biology lab.

"Eeeouw," exclaimed Louisa when she saw the enormous horse fly that Ginni had caught.

It was two inches long and buzzed in its jar like a deranged cell phone.

"Have a closer look," said Ginni. "Do you see the fly's eyes?"

"Yuck," said Louisa.

"This one is special," said Ginni. "It doesn't have two eyes; it has SIX THOUSAND eyes. Can you imagine having six thousand eyes? It's those eyes that make it so hard to catch a fly."

"That IS cool," admitted Louisa, her eyes widening as she bent over the insect.

Before long, Miss Butler announced they would have a science fair dedicated to creepy crawlies.

All the parents were invited to the fair, which was held in the school cafeteria. Ginni's stepmother had a migraine and couldn't come, but Ginni's father showed up.

The cafeteria was drab, with a gray linoleum floor, neon ceiling lights, and nondescript white walls. Each girl stood at her table, ready to explain her work. Near the cafeteria's entrance, Miss Butler had arranged a buffet with apple crumbles and custard tarts. There was also a large container with hot black tea, sugar, and cream in crystal containers, a tray with silver spoons, and delicate porcelain cups and plates.

Ginni showed off her extensive collection of photos of all the specimens she had cataloged. Each image had a label that included both the Latin and the ordinary names of the insect, worm, or spider, and some interesting tidbits about its biology, for example:

"Common house fly, Musca Domestica Linnaeus: Male house flies inject females with a drug that causes them to lose interest in sex, making them less likely to mate with other males."

Louisa had made a papier mache model of a hornet's nest. It showed the many layers of the nest's wall and the comb for the larvae. She had even found a few plastic hornets that she glued to the outside of the nest.

There was also a model of an insect eye, a demonstration of an earthworm dissection, and a collection of dung beetle pills.

The girls' parents were a little less enthusiastic than their daughters. There were loud and angry murmurs about firing Miss Butler and disenrolling their daughters. Only Ginni's father kept his cool.

"At least there are no live hornets," he said.

A week later, Ginni's father was summoned to meet with the principal, who tactfully suggested that perhaps this school wasn't the right fit for his lovely daughter.

Miss Butler was dismissed, but Lord Duggenham pulled a few strings, so she became headmistress at a boarding school for gifted children.

And Ginni? She went home and ran wild in the woods and on the beach again.

Five years passed; Ginni, now seventeen, still had her passion for bugs of all kinds. Ginni's stepmother was getting increasingly agitated about Ginni.

One day, at the dinner table, she blurted out, "Maybe we should send Ginni to ballroom dancing lessons. Ginny, you may meet a nice young man there."

The thought of dancing lessons made Ginni gag. Still, dancing lessons once a week were better than curtseying school every day.

Ginni's stepmother was adamant that Ginni be properly dressed for class and armed herself with make-up, hairspray, and nail polish. She procured a flowing blue dress embroidered with pearls and a pair of gold-colored shoes that nobody, but nobody, except perhaps Cinderella, could have walked in. She also insisted that Ginni put on a girdle that kept Ginni's belly from protruding.

Finally, the hour of the dancing lessons arrived, and Ginni hobbled towards the ballroom, her toes screaming in her tight shoes. Her manicured fingertips felt like plastic, and her head throbbed under the weight of a dozen hair clips.

The dancing instructor greeted the students at the entrance of the dance hall. He was a middle-aged, balding man with a heavy Italian accent. He looked all the girls up and down as they filed into the building. Ginni, noting that he was running his tongue over his large, brownish teeth, got a shiver down her spine.

The dance hall had a battered wooden floor and walls painted pale violet. There were a few tables and metal chairs. The light filtered through the dusty, yellowish shades of several table lamps.

The girls and the boys, all between seventeen and eighteen years old, were lined up on opposite walls. The boys wore tuxedos, red ties, and polished black shoes. They fidgeted and avoided eye contact. The girls all looked like porcelain dolls dressed in ankle-length satin gowns.

The dancing teacher grabbed one of the girls from her position at the wall and demonstrated how to hold onto a dancing partner.

Then, he showed the class the steps of a slow waltz while he sang the rhythm in his lilting Italian voice: "And a one and a two and a thrree, and a one and a two and a thrree."

"Now, find yourselves a partner, and let's danc-e," he said, turning on the music.

There were sixteen girls and fifteen boys. No one picked Ginni. As she stood there by herself at the wall, the instructor bowed before her.

"Mee-lady?"

He took Ginni by the hand and led her to the dance floor.

"And a one and a two and a thrree, and a one and a two and a thrree."

The instructor's hand on her shoulder blade was sweaty. The man smelled of red wine and garlic, and his pot belly pushed against Ginni's hips. Then, his fat hand wandered towards Ginni's waist.

"Excuse me," gasped Ginni and stepped hard on the instructor's foot.

While the teacher was doubling over and wincing, Ginni extricated herself from his grip, kicked off her shoes, and ran. She ran until she was out of breath, and the exertion had calmed her soul. She collapsed on a meadow near a foul-smelling pond that was three-quarters covered by algae. The meadow was wet from a recent rain, and the moisture soaked through Ginni's dress. She removed all the clips from her hair and unhooked the girdle.

As she sat there, still panting, she noticed a grasshopper. Then she saw that the pond was full of frogs practicing their evening serenades, and a garter snake slithered in the weeds. Ginni crawled on her hands and knees to catch the grasshopper and cupped it gently between her hands. Then she let it go.

"All life deserves to be protected," she whispered, then started to cry.

Ginni walked home barefoot. Her sky-blue dress was wet and covered with grass stains; only two of the twenty embroidered pearls were still in place.

Ginni's father sighed when he saw his daughter.

"Did you get yourself in trouble again?" he asked, frowning.

Ginni shook her head and said, "Dad, I don't want to go to that dancing school. Please. I can't."

"There is no discussion. You are a disappointment to me, Genevieve."

Ginni suppressed a sob and went to her room. When everybody slept, she snuck out of the house to escape to the beach. She sat down on the sand and watched the waves. The ocean was black as ink in the moonshine. The little waves seemed listless, with barely a crest. Dying jellyfish and starfish lay stranded near the high-tide line.

The quiet ocean was peaceful, though. All Ginni needed to do was wade into the water and swim straight ahead until her strength left her. No more girdles or nail polish, no more sweaty hands, no more disapproving looks, no more of the soul-crushing disappointment that emanated from her father. Ginni scrambled to her feet and walked towards the surf when she heard a voice behind her.

It was a young man carrying a bucket in his hand. He was the same age as Ginni, lanky, his dark hair cropped short. Ginni knew him from the stables, where he sometimes volunteered.

"Hello, Eric," said Ginni.

"Hello, Miss Ginni," said the boy.

The young man's bucket held a sea star, a few crabs, and a sand dollar, all alive in a bit of water.

"I am going to return those to the ocean," he said.

Eric walked up to the surf and released his catch, then he smiled at Ginni, "All the little creepy crawlies - there is a whole world out there that most people know nothing about."

"But you do?" Ginni asked skeptically, thinking it might be a ruse to get her to date this boy.

Eric hesitated, then blushed and said, "I have a whole collection of insect photos I took over the years. Everybody thinks I am a nerd."

"I want to see these photos!" Ginni exclaimed.

The following day, Ginni found her father in his study.

"We need to talk, Dad," said Ginni. "I will not go to that dancing school again. If you try to make me, I swear I am going to run away, and you will never see me again."

"Ginni!"

"I mean it."

"Let's go for a walk," said Ginni's father. "This study is stuffy."

Father and daughter crossed the drawbridge and walked down the gravel path into the forest.

"May I ask why you are so opposed to dancing lessons?" Ginni's father asked.

"Dad, this school is not about learning to dance. It's a meat market. I don't want to have to feel these groping hands on my body ever again."

Ginni's father was silent for a while, and then he said, "I am sorry, Ginni. I did not know."

"So, we are good?'

Lord Duggenham nodded and asked, "Where do you want to go to college, Ginni?"

"Newport. It has a college that offers a degree in entomology. And Eric is applying there, too."

*"Awwww," Fanny said. "Did Ginni become an entomologist?"*

*"Indeed, she did," said Michael. "And not just that. Ginni ended up marrying Eric. The wedding was something else. The reception hall was decorated with creepy crawlies of all kinds. The wedding cake looked like a giant crab. The bride and groom had donned little black hats with antennas and had transparent wings attached to their backs. The guests, too, wore insect costumes: Joseph was dressed as a bumblebee, and Ginni's father sat in the front row, wearing a June beetle suit, his eyes moist with happiness.*

*'Have you ever seen a prettier pair of entomologists?' he asked Miss Butler, who sat right beside him in her ladybug costume, holding Lord Duggenham's hand.*

*"What happened with Beatrice?" asked Fanny.*

*"Oh, she ran away with Ginni's tutor."*

# PART FIVE: REDEMPTION

# Chapter Thirty

# The Kiss of Death

Diana was old, and her time was near. She could no longer walk and was resting in her bed. Fanny was trying to spoon-feed her a little chicken broth, but the old woman gently pushed her away.

"Go have some fun," she told the girl. "I am not really hungry these days."

As she was arguing with Fanny, the bedroom door opened, and the Angel of Death stepped into the room.

"Go away," Fanny growled. "You can't have my Grandma."

The angel smiled at Fanny and said, "Boo."

"Give us some privacy, will you, Fanny?" Grandma said.

Fanny reluctantly left the room, leaving the door slightly ajar.

The old woman looked straight into Michael's eyes and asked, "Is it time?"

"Almost," the angel said.

"Michael," Diana said. "Could you lie down next to me, please?'

"Huh?" the angel said.

Diana scooted to the edge of the bed. "No touching - yet."

Michael stretched out on the bed next to Diana and closed his eyes.

Diana smiled at Michael. "I am going to give you a kiss. My mother told me that you never had one."

The angel opened his eyes and looked at Diana's wrinkly smile. To him, it was a radiant face of the purest beauty. Diana placed her lips on the angel's mouth and gave him a long, lingering kiss.

"How was that?" she asked when she was done.

"Marvelous," the angel said. "But how are you still alive?"

"I have thought about it," Diana explained. "Your touch ends life, and your breath restores life. A kiss is both touch and breath, so I was hoping that the effects might cancel each other out."

"Not once in ten thousand years did that occur to me!" the angel exclaimed.

He paused, then he added, "But it's still your time; I am sorry."

"I am not," Diana said.

At that moment, the bedroom door opened, and there was Fanny, who had been spying on them the whole time. Her face was tear-streaked, and her lips trembled as she looked at her grandmother, who was lying on her bed, side by side with the Angel of Death.

"Time to say goodbye to your grandma," Michael said.

Fanny took her grandmother in her embrace, kissed her, and whispered, "Goodbye, Grandma."

"Take good care of my angel," the old woman said. "He gets lonely."

Michael got up from Diana's bed and knelt at her bedside. He caressed the old woman's withered cheek, and she drew her last breath. In the hands of the angel, a delicate sphere took shape. It glowed in many colors, all intertwined in intricate patterns. The sphere hummed a melody that Fanny knew well.

The angel carefully lowered the soul into his gossamer bag and said, "Your grandmother had a most exquisite soul."

"Does my soul look like hers?" Fanny asked.

"One doesn't know what a soul will look like until the moment of death. Every day you live, every kindness you do, every hardship you suffer, all these things shape and color a soul."

At the funeral, Michael stood apart from the mourners. There were at least fifty people, all gathered around the open grave, huddled in winter coats and woolen hats.

The cemetery overlooked a snow-capped solitary mountain. On this day, the mountain was shrouded in mist; only its white summit rose over the fog. A small oak grove abutted the graveyard. The trees had let go of most of their leaves, and the gnarly shapes of trunks and branches stood silently against the wintry sky. Their discarded brown leaves floated into the open grave. Gusts of wind carried a frigid sprinkling of rain.

Fanny threw a shovelful of dirt on the casket. The casket was a simple box, made of rough wood and unadorned.

"Good-bye, Grandma," Fanny whispered, then she turned around and ran. Michael followed her to the wrought-iron cemetery gate, which depicted an angel holding a burning sword.

"Fanny," Michael said. "Grandma is at peace. She is asleep in the Space for Souls, and Jeema and Rowena are watching over her."

"Go away," Fanny sobbed. "You picked Grandma and me so that you could pretend to have a family, but I don't want you. Find a different family and get out of my sight, Angel of Death."

"I'll leave you alone," Michael said and took off into the windswept, icy sky.

A few days later, he was back.

He knocked at the door and asked, "Can I come in?"

"Do as you please," Fanny said. "Who can tell the Angel of Death what to do?"

"How are you, dear child?"

"I hate you," Fanny said. "Leave me alone. Everybody you touch dies."

Michael bowed his head and remained silent.

Fanny snorted, then she asked, "How do I find the Red Snake?"

"The Red Snake? Why on Earth would you want to find that thing?"

"Because. WHAT's its name?"

"Mephistopheles," Michael whispered. "But know that it cannot be trusted. Stay away from it if you value your soul."

"Thank you. I know how to take care of my soul," said Fanny as she marched through the door, slamming it shut.

Michael buried his face in his hands. "What have I done?"

# Chapter Thirty-One

# The Devil's Apprentice

Fanny walked until she came to an empty field, and then she yelled as loud as she could, "Mephistopheles, show yourself! Goddamn it, Mephistopheles, you scaly coward, COME to me."

Before Fanny's eyes, the air began to flicker, and the Red Snake made its appearance in a cloud of rust-colored dust.

"You called me, little girl?" asked the snake. "Are you ready to make a deal?"

"I am not a little girl, and I don't want to make a Stone King deal. But I will serve you as your apprentice if you show me the secrets of the world."

The snake pondered this request for a while, then it nodded its massive, red head and said, "You will serve me for seven years. In return, you will understand the balance of powers that govern this world."

Fanny suddenly had a hard time breathing. Pain was searing through her body as it stretched out and grew scales. Her body grew wiry and strong. Fanny's tongue became forked and now served as her nose, able to smell prey from a mile away. Two gleaming white fangs erupted from her upper jaw. The scales on Fanny's back formed a zigzagging pattern of yellow and black.

Fanny's voice hissed as she said, "So, now I am a snake, like you. What's next?"

"First things first," said Mephistopheles. "The first thing is dinner."

Fanny followed the Red Snake, slithering through the field as if she had done this sort of thing all her life. The tall grasses obscured her vision, but her tongue picked up a world of scents. She knew of every mouse in the field, every horsefly, and every frog. Her body was strong and firm, made to be coiled, to strike, and devour.

Mephistopheles did not stop until they reached a farmhouse in the valley.

"Now we wait," said the Red Snake.

It did not take long, and an old man stumbled through the farmhouse door. He was clutching his chest, whimpering softly to himself. Then, when he saw the two snakes, his whimpering became wails.

"Stone King!" he yelled with the last of his strength.

The Red Snake swept upon the dying man and sank its fangs into his body. When the man lay still, his soul separated from the corpse and tumbled onto the grass. The small sphere was entirely covered with stone, and when the sunlight hit it, it disintegrated into a pile of sand.

"Eat," said the Red Snake as it licked up the sand. "Eat. Eating souls is your education."

"How so?" asked Fanny.

"Each soul contains the wisdom and learning of its full lifetime, and you will absorb all of that into yourself."

"He is dead?" asked Fanny. "So, I won't hurt him, correct?"

"Correct," nodded Mephistopheles, and Fanny began to lick at the sand.

Each grain of sand infused Fanny with a surge of energy. Her snake body grew fatter, and her scales became more lustrous.

"I see all the mysteries!" she exclaimed.

"No, you don't understand the world yet," said Mephistopheles. "You just feel like you do. You will have to eat many more souls to get a true understanding."

"I want a nap," said Fanny later when the soul-high wore off, and tiredness swept over her body. "Please?"

Mephistopheles nodded and found a hiding place in the tall grass where Fanny could sleep.

The next lesson was different. Mephistopheles ambushed a frightened child and offered him the Stone King deal.

"He does not HAVE to invoke the Stone King, right?" asked Fanny.

"No, but they all do."

"Humans have choices, don't they?" mused Fanny. "So, it's their own fault if they lose their souls."

"Free will is an illusion," muttered the Red Snake under its breath.

For seven years, Fanny followed the Red Snake, shared its meals, and watched it frighten young children. Then, one day, as the two snakes were about to devour a soul, Michael stumbled upon them.

"Fanny!" exclaimed Michael when he saw the black and yellow, very fat snake. "What have you done?"

Fanny eyed Michael coldly and said, "I am fine, Godfather Death. Leave me alone."

"Fanny, please," stammered Michael. "Don't tell me you are now hunting for souls?"

"You soft-hearted idiot," snarled Fanny. "Souls are for eating. What do you think Earth will do with all the souls you are saving for her?"

"Well, isn't this cute - a little reunion?" said the Red Snake as it devoured the pile of soul sand in the grass. "Anyway, Fanny, much as I enjoyed your company, it's been seven years, and it's time to part ways."

"Then, make me human again," said Fanny.

The Red Snake flicked its tongue and shook its head, "No."

"It can't turn you back into your human form," whispered Michael. "All the souls you have eaten have compromised your soul. You no longer have a fully human soul."

The Red Snake laughed, "There is always a price to pay, isn't there, Michael?"

The snake slithered closer to Michael and lifted its head until its forked tongue almost touched Michael's face; then it said, "What price will you pay, Michael, if I may ask?"

"What do you mean?" asked Michael, blanching and backing away from the snake.

"What was it like to be kissed by a woman?" snickered the Red Snake. "Did you enjoy yourself?"

The Angel of Death looked stricken.

"It was one kiss," he stuttered. "Just one kiss."

"You know that I killed and ate all the other angels because they fell in love with humans, don't you?" hissed the Red Snake.

"Yes," Michael said in a small voice.

"I will feast on you, Angel of Death. As soon as I get permission from Earth."

Michael straightened his back and looked the Red Snake in the eye.

"Earth is my master," said Michael. "My master's judgment I will accept, however harsh it may be."

"We'll see what we'll see," hissed the Red Snake, then it slithered away.

"What about me?" yelled Fanny. "I don't want to remain a snake."

"It's too late," whispered Michael.

The angel started to cry, and his tears dripped on the ground where the sandy remains of the soul had been spilled. One of Michael's tears fell on a single grain of the soul sand, and a translucent, small sphere appeared in the grass. It had a dim glow and no markings of any kind. Michael cupped the tiny soul in his hands, and a smile spread over his face.

"A baby soul! It's from the soul you consumed, Fanny. It will have another chance. It can be reborn in a brand-new body."

"Can I have it?" asked Fanny, flicking her tongue to smell the little sphere. "I am hungry."

"You can never again eat a soul," said Michael.

While Michael put the baby soul in his carrying bag, Fanny suddenly doubled over, gasping.

Michael took a close look at Fanny's snake face and said, "Your eyes are no longer yellow and slit. They are green now and full of emotions. You have your human eyes back, Fanny." He paused, then he muttered, "Maybe…"

"Maybe what?"

"Do you remember the places where you ate all those souls? If you can lead me to these places, and if I can find as much as a single grain of sand in each of these locations, you may get your humanity back."

The next day, Fanny and Michael traveled to an oak grove where Fanny had feasted on a soul not two weeks before. Fanny's slithering was slow and clumsy. Her scales had lost their luster, and small purulent pustules had formed near her head. When they arrived at the grove, Fanny collapsed on the ground, shaking and whimpering with pain.

"What's wrong?" asked Michael.

"I am hungry. I told you, I am hungry."

"Well, what do you eat?" asked Michael. "I may be able to get a few rats for you."

Fanny howled, "I need a soul. You have plenty of souls in your carrying bag. Give me just one. Nobody will miss it."

"I can't do that," said Michael.

Fanny reared up and opened her jaws, revealing gleaming white fangs. She hissed at Michael, dousing him with her putrescent breath. Then she got ready to strike the angel, but stopped.

"I'll kill you. Give me a soul," she shrieked.

Michael shook his head and sat on the grass, near Fanny but out of reach of her fangs. Fanny groaned and wheezed; then, her skin split lengthwise. She squirmed her way out of the old hide, gasping with the effort. Her new skin was as dull as the one she had shed and covered with pus. Fanny moaned weakly; then she passed out.

Michael searched between the trees and found a few grains of soul sand. His tears came easily to him; all he needed to do was look at the unconscious snake stretched out on the ground like a dried-up, dead earthworm.

Fanny was subdued when she came to, and Michael noticed that some blonde hair was sprouting on her snake head.

"Better?" asked Michael.

"Hungry," replied Fanny.

"Would you like a rat?" asked Michael.

"Fine," grumbled Fanny and devoured five rats that Michael had brought in a little carrying cage.

"Where did you get the rats?" Fanny wanted to know.

"From a pet store," said Michael, blushing. "I stole them."

Michael and Fanny went on to the next place where Fanny remembered eating a soul. While the sun was overhead, Fanny held it together, but when night came, she shivered and thrashed around. Sleep eluded her for hours, and when she finally did fall asleep, she had nightmares, from which she woke up screaming and ramming her fangs in the dirt.

The snake and the angel continued their slow journey for months. Michael cried until his eyes were red and dry.

Little by little, Fanny became more human. When her fangs fell out, her craving for souls abated. Before long, Fanny's mouth grew red lips.

Michael supplied Fanny with a steady supply of rats, but one day, she distorted her face in disgust.

"I can't eat this," she exclaimed. "Don't you have any real food? Human food?"

Michael hurried back to the city where he had stolen the rats and returned to Fanny with a paper bag full of groceries.

"Cheesecake," he said. "That used to be your favorite. With raspberries on top and whipped cream."

Fanny's eyes lit up, and she sank her face into the cake, slurping up cheesecake.

"Sorry for the messy eating," she said. "I wish I had hands."

Then she paused and added, "Would you like some cake, Michael?"

Michael nodded and broke off a corner of the cake that was not covered with Fanny's saliva.

In time, Fanny lost most of her scales. Then, she grew shoulders and arms, followed by legs, hands, and feet, and her tail shriveled away.

There was only one more location left to check out. Fanny remembered it well. It was near the farmhouse where she had consumed her first soul. Alas, even Michael could not find a single grain of soul sand in the grass.

Fanny looked almost human now, with just a patch of yellow and black scales on her back.

"I am afraid this is the best I can do," admitted Michael after searching the grass for hours. "You can now pass for human, but your soul remains defective. When your body dies, it will disintegrate and be lost forever."

Hearing this, Fanny sat down on the grass and sobbed.

"I am so sorry, Michael," she whispered. "This is all my fault."

"There is only one more thing that we can try," sighed Michael. "And it means that I have to request an audience with Earth and accept my judgment."

"For that one kiss?"

"Yes," said Michael. "Will you come with me, Fanny? I must admit I am a bit scared."

"The Angel of Death is intimidated!" Fanny smiled. "It will be okay, Michael. And I will come with you even if we must go to the end of the world."

# Chapter Thirty-Two

# Judgment Day

"Let's go then," said Michael, and darkness, as thick as molasses, fell over the field. When it lifted, Michael and Fanny stood in a forest of ancient, moss-covered trees. Pale strands of lichen hung from the twigs, and a fine mist wafted between the branches. A thundering waterfall cascaded over a cliff nearby.

"This way," said Michael as he led Fanny up the slippery rocks towards the hidden cave behind the waterfall. The mist made Fanny's blonde hair cling to her face. She wiped a few locks from her eyes and stopped at the entrance of the gloomy cavern; then, she stepped into the dark. The angel and the young woman followed a short path through the cave and emerged in a shadow-filled clearing.

"Behold, the Great Audience Hall of the Spirit of Earth," said Michael.

Before them, the branches of smooth, silver-barked trees formed a high roof, creating a space as otherworldly as a cathedral. The clearing was silent. Not even the insects were buzzing, and the brilliantly colored birds in the canopy seemed to hold their breath. The only sound was the muffled rush from the waterfall behind them. Fanny and Michael walked across luminous moss towards the large, polished tree stump that marked the center of the clearing.

Michael stopped at a respectful distance from the stump and whispered to Fanny, "Now, we wait. Do as I do."

A brief time later, the Red Snake appeared. It was fatter and more lustrous than Michael ever remembered. It slithered towards the tree stump and wrapped itself around it twice.

For what seemed like hours, nothing happened. The silence was thick under the trees. Then, the air crackled, the colors of the vegetation intensified, and the soft rushing of the waterfall turned into thunder.

Michael fell to his knees, bowing his head.

"I don't see anybody," Fanny whispered to Michael.

"She is here, but not in her visible form."

Fanny hesitated for a moment, then knelt next to Michael and lowered her head. The presence of Earth was palpable. It descended on Fanny like a warm blanket, enfolding her body and covering her face. For a moment, Fanny struggled to breathe, but she realized quickly that the ghostly embrace did not want to harm her.

The Red Snake uncoiled itself and reared up until its head hovered ten feet above Michael and Fanny. Small droplets of poison formed on the tip of its fangs and dripped to the ground.

The snake spat out its accusation, "Spirit of Earth, the Angel of Death has betrayed you. He allowed himself to fall in love with a human and accepted her kiss."

The snake turned to Michael and hissed, "Is this not the truth, Angel of Death?"

"Yes, it is," said Michael, still kneeling and looking down at the ground.

"I request permission to terminate this pathetic creature," the Red Snake demanded.

"Michael," Fanny whispered. "There is more to the story. Tell them."

"It was one kiss," Michael said, lifting his eyes toward the center of the clearing. "That kiss was the dying wish of a woman I loved. You would have me refuse it?"

"The Angel of Death is forbidden from having carnal relations with humans," the snake snarled. "He is a tool, soulless and meant for one purpose only - to collect souls. A defective tool must be destroyed and replaced."

"Great Spirit of Earth," Michael said. "Please hear me. I fear you. My life is but a flickering candle in your hands."

Michael paused, then he continued, "I also love you, Mother of All. When I need comfort or guidance, I turn to you because I have no one else. Disobedience to you is the last thing of which I would ever want to be guilty."

Michael closed his eyes. "Yet, I could not refuse that kiss. And what's worse, I wanted it. I wanted it more than anything in the world."

The Red Snake flicked its tongue over the rim of its mouth.

Michael took a deep breath and said, "Mother of All, I failed you. I failed my family, too. I was wrong to extend Jeema's life. I brought misery on her and her offspring.

"What comes next, Great Spirit of Earth, I deserve. But, if my ten thousand years of faithful service have pleased you, would you grant me one wish?"

"Speak your wish," echoed a voice that seemed to come from every direction.

"Help Fanny," the Angel of Death whispered.

"No, no, no, no!" Fanny exclaimed. "Don't use your one wish on me. I'll be OK. Ask for a pardon, Michael."

"Step forward, Michael," Earth said.

Michael got up from his knees and approached the center of the clearing.

"Please, show me your face," he pleaded.

A soft mist arose from the ground, and in the fog, the Spirit of Earth took shape. She appeared as a tall, dark woman with long white hair down to her hips. She was clad in a moss-green robe, and in her right hand, she held her white staff.

A timid smile spread over Michael's face.

"I am ready," he whispered.

Earth pulled Michael closer, and the angel stood motionless in her embrace. Earth pressed her dark hand into Michael's chest and reached for his heart. He trembled, then he uttered a small, painful cry and collapsed. He lay still on the muddy ground, his eyes wide open, staring at the patches of sky between the tree branches.

"Michael!" Fanny yelled.

She ran to Michael's side and picked him up in her arms, not caring if touching the angel might bring about her own death.

"Michael, no."

A luminous sphere took shape in Earth's hand.

"Please, forgive him," Fanny cried.

"Would you like to hold his soul?" Earth asked.

Fanny lowered Michael's body to the ground and held out her hands to receive his soul. The sphere was warm and soft to the touch. It had a bright glow, and delicate patterns of blue and purple swam across its surface. It quivered in Fanny's hands.

"It's not singing," Fanny said. "Why is it not singing?"

"It's scared," Earth said. "Scared souls do not sing."

"There, there," Fanny whispered, stroking the soul while she cradled it against her chest. "Don't be frightened. As long as I live, I will always be there for you."

"That's a big promise to make for a mere human," Earth remarked.

"I mean it," Fanny wept. "My grandmother asked me to take good care of her angel, but I didn't. Instead, I caused him such heartache, such grief."

As Fanny comforted the soul, the luminescent sphere stopped trembling, and Fanny thought she heard a faint hum.

When the hum became louder, Fanny smiled through her tears, "I remember this music. It's the melody that came from my Grandma's soul when Michael held it in his hands."

"I think you should now put this soul back where it belongs," Earth said.

"How?"

"Place it on Michael's mouth. It will find its way from there."

Fanny carefully set the sphere on Michael's pale lips. The sphere lost its rigid shape and began to flow into the angel's mouth. When it had vanished, Michael took a deep, ragged breath and sat up. His eyes were wild until he saw Fanny's face.

"Fanny! I had the weirdest dream," he gasped. "I was a soul, and you were holding me in your hands. And I never wanted you to let go of me."

"Ahem," said a voice behind Michael.

Michael was startled. "Earth, I am so sorry. I forgot where I was."

He tried to scramble to his feet, but his legs would not support him, and he fell back to the ground. Fanny smiled at the sight of the bedraggled angel, who sat there in the mud, his feathers ruffled, his hair falling over his face in disorderly strands, and his clothes and plumage streaked with dirt.

"Rest for a minute," Earth said to Michael. "Anyway, where was I? Ah, yes, the Red Snake was wrong about Michael, as we have seen. This angel has grown himself a soul. - And a fine little soul it is."

"I have a soul?" Michael asked. "How?"

"I think it was Grandma's kiss," Fanny whispered. "Didn't you tell me that women can share a sliver of their souls with the men they love?"

"I have a soul! I did not know I had a soul. I always wanted a soul."

"Get used to it," said Fanny.

In the meantime, Earth turned to the snake and said, "But you, Mephistopheles, are indeed soulless, created only to put fear in the hearts of women and men. And you have transgressed."

The Red Snake opened its jaws and displayed its enormous fangs. "How have I gone astray, Spirit of Earth? I did what I was created to do. Would you blame me for it?"

"You deceived and corrupted a pure and innocent soul," Earth said. "I did not give you that authority. Be gone, Red Snake. I do not want to see your face on the surface of the planet for ten thousand years. Find a cave to hide in and ponder your arrogance."

The Red Snake disappeared in a cloud of rust-colored dust, and Earth turned her attention to Fanny.

"You, child, are both courageous and stupid as humans are wont to be."

Fanny felt a light wind blow over her, and she knew that the scales on her back were gone. A sense of well-being and wholeness coursed through her body.

"Now to you, Michael," Earth said with a smile in her eyes. "I forgive you, as your human companion has asked, but there is a penance to pay: From now on, you will be tasked with taking care of the souls in the Beyond. Many of them are scared and alone. Comfort them as only the Angel of Death and his companion can comfort a soul."

"His companion?!" Fanny exclaimed. "Yes, I will help!"

Then she paused and added, "If a mere human can do this job."

"I can make arrangements," Earth said.

"Do I still have my death angel's duties?" asked Michael, who had managed to get up on his shaky legs by holding on to one of the trees.

"Yes, indeed, and don't pretend I am overworking you."

Michael shook his head, "No," and looked down at his feet.

"Do you have something else on your mind?" asked Earth, her voice gentle and soft.

The birds in the canopy of the ancient trees chirped to one another, a light wind rustled the leaves, and the bumblebees hummed among the fragrant flowers.

"Could I be so bold?" Michael stuttered.

"Go ahead."

"Please, bring the angels back," Michael blurted out. "I miss them."

"You miss them even though they wanted nothing to do with you? Even though they spurned you for having the touch of death?"

Michael nodded, "Yes, please."

Laughter, like the gurgling of a small brook, filled the room between the tall trees.

"As you wish, my dark Angel of Mercy. The Angels of Light can help you in the Beyond."

Earth chuckled, "And, for the sake of brave little Fanny, I will remove Michael's curse: From now on, Michael can will himself to be heard and seen, and his touch will no longer bring death unless he desires it so."

Earth paused, then she laughed, "Don't go overboard, though, Michael. One girl at a time. Now be gone, both of you."

The Audience Hall disappeared, and Michael and Fanny found themselves in the meadow near Diana's old hut. Michael's gleaming, raven-black wings scintillated in the light of the moon. His smooth, black hair framed a clean-shaven face with sensuous lips and luminous blue eyes. Fanny's blonde locks cascaded over her shoulders down to the small of her back. Her body was as soft and as young as the dawn that approached in the East.

As Michael and Fanny looked at each other, a warm light appeared near the edge of the meadow, but it was not the rising sun. It grew brighter and brighter until it flooded the field. The outlines of winged creatures appeared in the brilliance. Then, sweet, soft singing arose.

"The angels," Michael said. "The Angels of Light are back."

The music continued for several minutes, then the light faded, and the field lay in twilight again. Fanny and Michael were bathed in the early glow of dawn.

9 798999 343017